War Is . . .

WAR IS...

Soldiers, Survivors, and Storytellers Talk About War

edited by

MARC ARONSON

and

PATTY CAMPBELL

CANDLEWICK PRESS

To the men and women who served in combat during my lifetime. I hope that in this book, we who were at home and you who were in battle can begin to see, hear, and heal one another. I owe a special debt to every one of you who told me your story, and whose words are here. Thank you for letting me listen.

M. A.

Dedicated to my sons—Fred, Broos, and Cameron—who never had to fight a war, and to their sons—Brendan, Clay, Chad, Chase, and Cory—with the hope that neither will they.

P. C.

Compilation copyright © 2008 by Marc Aronson and Patty Campbell
"War Is . . . ? An Introduction by Patty Campbell" copyright © 2008 by Patty Campbell
"People Like War: An Introduction by Marc Aronson" copyright © 2008 by Marc Aronson

Copyright acknowledgments appear on pages 276–77.

First paperback edition 2009

The Library of Congress has cataloged the hardcover edition as follows:

Aronson, Marc, and Patty Campbell.

War is . . . : soldiers, survivors, and storytellers talk about war / edited by Marc Aronson and Patty Campbell. —1st ed.

p. cm.
Summary: An anthology of fiction, speeches, poems, and essays about war.
ISBN 978-0-7636-3625-8 (hardcover)
[1. War—Literary collections. 2. American literature—20th century.] I. Title.
PS509.W3 W37 2008
810.8—dc22   2007052026

ISBN 978-0-7636-4231-0 (paperback)

1 2 3 4 5 6 7 8 9 10

Printed in the United States of America

This book was typeset in Granjon.

Candlewick Press
99 Dover Street
Somerville, Massachusetts 02144

visit us at www.candlewick.com

*"If I were King of the World,
I'd make a rule that there
would be no more wars.
No fighting, any place, ever—
except when I say so."*

—Simon Cohen, seven years old

CONTENTS

WHAT I BELIEVE ABOUT WAR

WAR IS . . . ?

an introduction by Patty Campbell

WAR IS . . .

CRAZY. Looked at without its veil of noble causes and glory, war is insanity, as Mark Twain so deftly observes in "The War Prayer," a story that was deemed so controversial that it was not published until many years after his death. For the people of one country to try to kill as many of the people of another country as possible makes no sense at all, in terms of our common humanity. Yet . . .

WAR IS . . .

HISTORY. The story of civilization has always been told in terms of a progression of wars. We have always waged war against one another, and the leaders of those wars are the people who are praised or deplored in our memories. The artists, the composers, the architects, the actors and dancers, the women and children, daily life and religion—these matters we leave to the archaeologists and the anthropologists to record. But it is the kings and warriors who are remembered in the history books.

WAR IS . . .

DECEPTION. Even in conventional warfare, the first thing that must happen before a nation can be led to war is to demonize the enemy, to portray those others as less than human. Stories begin to be shared about their dreadful deeds, and derogatory terms replace their true names. Soldiers cannot be allowed to remember that the people they will be sent to kill feel pain and fear and love their spouses and children, just as *they* do. And even the U.S. government's enlistment contract is shockingly deceptive, as Bill Bigelow warns in "The Recruitment Minefield," his revelation of recruitment activities with high-school students. Nor can civilians be allowed to know the real causes of war. Slogans like "to preserve freedom" and "to protect the world for democracy" sometimes mask the actual economic and political incentives.

WAR IS . . .
UNBEARABLE. The ugly details of how people die in war and the brutality of battle is often more than the psyche can endure. People see things in war that the human soul is not equipped to bear. In every war, many soldiers return wounded not in their bodies but in their minds. After the Civil War, this condition was referred to as "soldier's heart." Now we describe it as "post-traumatic stress disorder." Battle veterans almost invariably carry emotional and psychological scars.

WAR IS . . .
DELUSION. The bait that entices young people to become soldiers is glory, as we see in the reflections

of students at the grave of a young marine in the article that opens this collection. The reward of medals and honor and a sense of patriotic duty and loyalty to comrades cover the ugly reality that a soldier's primary job is to kill and destroy. While it is old men who plan the wars, the dying and killing has always been done by the young, as Bob Dylan rages against in his song "Masters of War."

WAR IS . . .

MALE. Although there have been exceptions— Joan of Arc, Elizabeth I, the Celtic warrior queen Boadicea—the leaders of war have nearly always been men. For most of history, it has been women who weep for their dead sons and husbands, women who are the victims of rape and enslavement, while men fight and die on the battlefield. Editor Marc Aronson has brought the unhappy experiences of women in the military to this anthology with Helen Benedict's "Women at War," an essay on what it's like to be a female soldier in Iraq, while my own father's World War I letters from Paris, "Letters from 'Over There,'" show the typical horsing around of young men having fun, even in the presence of war.

WAR IS . . .

LINKED WITH RELIGION. The sad fact is that throughout history religion has provided motivation and support for many wars. But on the other hand, some churches, like the Religious Society of Friends, or Quakers, find a rationale in their faith for acting out peace. And some young men, as Chaplain Lyn Brown describes in his interview with me, "Thou Shalt Not Kill," move to become conscientious objectors when confronted with the realities of battle.

WAR IS . . .
WORSE FOR CIVILIANS. The devastation of war is always harder on civilians than it is on soldiers, and civilian casualties vastly outnumber those suffered by the military. For instance, while the U.S. lost 58,000 soldiers in Vietnam, it is estimated that more than three million Vietnamese civilians died from war-related causes. And at this present writing, U.S. deaths in Iraq number at least 4,000, while Iraqi civilian deaths exceed 78,000 (although a recent study by Johns Hopkins University published in the respected medical journal *The Lancet* estimates the number at 655,000).

War also often destroys a society's most basic means of survival, its ability to provide food and shelter, water and electricity, as well as the delicate psychological and moral structures that hold a civilization together with the authority of law and the expectation of safety and mutual dependency, as we see in Margo Lanagan's stunning story

"Heads" and Fumiko Miura's memoir of the day the atomic bomb was dropped on Nagasaki.

WAR IS . . .
IMPOSSIBLE TO WIN. Modern warfare takes the form of terrorism, and this is a type of war we don't know how to fight. The insurgent army's soldiers wear no uniforms and are indistinguishable from the general population—until they shoot. There are no battlefields, no occupied territory, no visible enemy, and no possibility of victory. Yet we continue to fight this new kind of war as if all these features from the past were still in place, a failed strategy that makes it inevitable that there will be no endpoint for hostilities.

WAR IS . . .
INEVITABLE? The fact that humans have always waged war in the past leads many people to theorize that we will always wage war in the future. They argue that it is a biological imperative, bred in our genes. However, we are born with many other antisocial impulses that must be overcome before we can live together in civilization, and we have been able to do so. Certainly if we see the impulse to war clearly and understand its origins, we can begin to encourage our children to actively seek peace instead.

As a first step, young people considering the

military as an option need to have the realities of war clearly revealed to them in many different voices so that they can make a decision based on truth. I have gathered pieces for this anthology with that essential goal in mind, and I make no secret of the fact that they reflect my passionate revulsion toward war.

PEOPLE LIKE WAR

an introduction by Marc Aronson

People like war. There is only one thing we like better: sex. War and sex: human history. War and sex seem like opposites—love versus hate, creation versus destruction, life versus death. But their bond goes deeper than that. Chris Hedges ("The Moment of Combat") was a newspaper reporter who worked in one miserable war zone after another. He lived through scenes that the rest of us experience only in our worst nightmares. I really mean that. He learned how grim war is, and that it is far, far worse than people living in their peaceful homes ever know. But he also understood something else: people like war; no, they love it.

I recently met with some neighbors, both thoughtful, deeply caring people. She is a psychologist who counsels people who have suffered through the most terrible crimes in war. He is a businessman. But he described his time of serving in dangerous combat in Vietnam as "when I felt most alive."

Chris reports that in war, every second matters. In war, soldiers and civilians fall in love—love that lasts only as long as the war. War strips people down to basics: Will I live? Will I win? Will I conquer? Will I be defeated? but also: me, you, no future, no past, now.

I have never been in a war, so I have to take Chris's word for it. I was living in Manhattan on September 11, 2001, though, and I remember the intensity he speaks of. We were all afraid, so we all drew closer. Strangers talked to each other, helped each other. We sang together; we came alive.

People like Chris who have seen war say that we civilians have it wrong—or worse, that war as we see it is a lie. They say war as we see it in books and movies is false, a cover-up. When I was growing up, that was true—we played cowboys and Indians, we read Captain America comics, we watched heroic World War II movies. But today, movies, TV, graphic novels, and books often go out of their way to avoid glamorizing war. And yet I am sure that we civilians still have it wrong. That is because liking war does not just come from what the media tells us; it comes from inside us.

We crave combat. We yearn for victory. Look at gamers in front of their screens: they don't *want* to kill monsters and aliens; they *need* to. War is a drug. Read the interviews before any championship—the Super Bowl, the World Series, the Indy 500, the NBA finals, the NCAA Final Four, not to mention boxing matches—surely someone will say, "We are going to war." In high-school locker rooms throughout the country, the world, athletes say precisely the same thing. We invented those games; they are extremely popular. We don't say, "We are going to cooperate. We are going to make friends. We are going to spread peace and harmony." We say, "We are going to war." We say that because we want to experience war. We want it so much we play at it when we cannot have it.

And *we* means all of us. If you have any doubt that women are drawn to combat, read any novel about two girls, teenagers, or adult women competing for a prize, a school vote, a romantic interest. You will always see the language of hatred, annihilation—in fact, war. And while traditionally men fight wars, women often share the same views of the enemy and transmit them in songs and stories to their children. A Muslim student from Bosnia with whom I went to graduate school predicted the entire horrible war that soon took so many lives in his country. The stories Serbian, Croatian, and Bosnian mothers tell, he warned, nurse hatreds going back centuries. All over the world, mothers have reared their sons to be warriors, to be killers, to fight.

So if we like war, we need to know more about it. Young adult sections of bookstores and libraries are filled with novels, self-help books, and graphic novels on teens' changing bodies, dating, and safe sex. There is no YA section on war. There are a few novels, the occasional memoir, and some teenagers are motivated enough to go to adult shelves. This book grew out of a panel discussion in which Harry Mazer, Paul Fleischman, Jim Murphy, and Walter Dean Meyers talked about their experiences of war, and how they then wrote about it for teenagers. That panel is available at www.candlewick.com. Margo Lanagan and Rita Williams-Garcia have pieces in this anthology. But the overwhelming reality of portrayals of war in YA literature is a killing silence. We like war, and we pretend it doesn't exist. And yet it is teenagers who make up the next generation of soldiers and civilians. Both fighters and those at home need to know what they are in for.

I have never faced the choice of whether to serve in combat. During the Vietnam War, I was of draft age, but I was in college, and my number was low enough that I was never called. I did not have to choose. Today I have two young sons, and I pray they won't face death in combat. Yet I know in my guts that something is wrong in how we deal with war and service. Everyone I know is completely insulated from fighting. No one, none of us who edit, design, produce, market, or review this book will have served in the military. And we are all equally determined to keep our children safe. We are a divided country in which many people will go to any length to keep war, to keep the entire military world, far, far away.

When I began looking for entries to place in this book, I was especially interested in heroism, sacrifice, the community of friendship that can come from serving in war. You will see these themes in some of the pieces I found, but along the way I learned something I knew intellectually but had never truly understood: everyone pays a price for being in war, winners as well as losers. For some, for Patty, my coeditor, that means we should not fight wars. But I came to a different conclusion: if we ask people to fight for us—as we always have and always will—we owe them the respect of listening to them. We have to honor their experience by paying attention to it, no matter how uncomfortable it makes us. They have the right to curse at us, at life, at fate; they have the right to be bitter; they have the right to nurse their wounds. As Joel Turnipseed, author of the selection "Tough," said to me, something dies in you when you fight in a war. If we ask soldiers to suffer that wound, we must listen as they try to regain their humanity. That is what we owe them.

The great World War II reporter Ernie Pyle describes the men on D-day—their terror, and their choice, their decision, to face the enemy. Every soldier must face that crossing point— I fear, I must. When do the rest of us have such stark choices—confessing a secret, confronting a bully, challenging a teacher? Caught up in our own world, sealed off from theirs, we are blind, totally blind, to the choices soldiers face. We view war as wrong, misguided, an error that should not take place.

I believe that is our big mistake. We say a particular war is wrong—in Iraq, the Persian Gulf,

Vietnam. But I am certain that the United States will go to war again, and again, and again. I believe that is a fact of our lives, of all human lives. And since we will go to war, soldiers will again, and again, and again face that moment of decision—I fear, I must. And many of those soldiers will die.

Hating war makes it too easy to avoid really looking at war itself. And so in this collection, I set out to find pieces from people who have served in war (Mickey Andrews, C. W. Bowman, Christian Bauman, Lee Kelley, Joel Turnipseed), have covered war (Ernie Pyle, Chris Hedges, Helen Benedict), or grew up in military families (Rita Williams-Garcia). I looked for honesty about war—in all of its aspects. Make of this book what you will, but at least you will have heard directly from those who have faced that fire.

DECIDING ABOUT WAR

DEAD MARINE BECOMES LESSON FOR STUDENTS

This Associated Press story appeared in many newspapers on Memorial Day, 2007. The reporter is unattributed.

ARLINGTON, VA (MAY 28)—Just a few years ago, Lance Cpl. Steven Szwydek was a classmate of students at a high school in the mountains of Pennsylvania's Fulton County. Now the fallen Marine is part of their history lesson. On separate days this spring, students from all three high schools in his home county visited Arlington National Cemetery, where they stopped for a moment of silence at his white tombstone. The bus trips were paid for by a memorial fund established by Szwydek's parents.

Their quiet son—a history buff who loved to hunt deer—was 20 when he was killed in 2005 by a roadside bomb during his second tour of Iraq.

His mother, Nancy Szwydek, is a strong supporter of President Bush and the Iraq war but said the trips are not about politics or trying to influence students to join the military. She and her husband don't accompany the classes on the trips.

She sees the annual visits as a way to teach students "to respect our freedom." Teachers say the trips are as much about establishing connections—

between kids growing up in a rural county and world events.

Nancy and Michael Szwydek, who own a country store, decided a college scholarship in their son's name would not have made sense because he chose the Marines over college. "I think he would not want himself being the focus . . . but I think he'd be real happy the students have had a history lesson," Nancy Szwydek said during an interview at her home in Warfordsburg, Pennsylvania, near the Maryland border.

For some of the students, the stop at Szwydek's grave is personal because they attended school with him at Southern Fulton Junior/Senior High. They recalled seeing their teachers cry the day it was learned he had died.

"It was very nice of them to let us experience this, and we're supporting Steven and that's the main reason we're down here," said Miranda Blackburn, 17, during her visit to Arlington.

A student from another high school, Kirstie Barton, also 17, said the cemetery brings home the reality of the war.

"It's kind of hard to grasp that people go over there and they die every day and their families are missing them," she said.

Tim Mills, 17, said two relatives have served in Iraq and he is considering joining the Pennsylvania National Guard.

"If I die, I die. There's no stopping that. That's God's plan. Just, that's how I look at it. I'm ready to go. Maybe I'll be here one day," he said.

Angie Booth, a teacher from Szwydek's school who helped lead one of the trips, grew up next to him and baby-sat him.

She pointed out to her students that since a school trip last year, two new rows of graves of soldiers killed in Iraq had been added near Szwydek's. Some were so fresh they didn't have tombstones yet—just flowers.

Booth said she wants the students to learn that, "even though we're a very rural community, we're not isolated from this either."

Szwydek joined the Marines when he was 17, leaving for boot camp four days after graduating from high school.

On his original paperwork, he wrote that he wanted to be buried at sea.

"I said, 'Steven, why do you want to be buried at sea?' At this time, it was a joke," said Nancy Szwydek.

"He said, 'No special reason, Mom, I just thought it would be cool.' And I said, 'Change it,' so he just put 'buried with full military honors.'"

LETTER TO A YOUNG ENLISTEE

by Christian Bauman

Christian Bauman is the author of the novels In Hoboken, Voodoo Lounge, *and* The Ice Beneath You. *He served in the U.S. Army Waterborne from 1991 to 1995, including tours in Somalia and Haiti.*

June 2007

Let's get right to the point—anything I say to you here has to answer your biggest question: "Should I or shouldn't I join the military?" Everything else is just crap, right? *Time's a wasting, and I need to know: Should I or shouldn't I?*

Well, let me submit this to you: I believe you've already made the decision. You're only here looking to validate your decision.

Am I right?

Really. Stop and think hard. Am I right?

You know what it is you're going to do, don't you?

Joining the military is one of the most profound and personal decisions you'll ever make. Up there with who you'll marry. And I have to tell you right here: I'm not going to help you make the decision. First of all, because—as I've already said—I think the decision has been made. Hasn't it? But second of all, I'm just not going to help.

"What a cop-out," you're saying. Or, as translated into army speak, "What a fucking pussy this guy is." (That phrase is just as likely to come from a female soldier as a male; you'll get used to it.)

"What a jerk," you might be saying right now. "Some tough guy author—goes to war, says he's a soldier, writes about it. But can't even go on record for or against. Some tough guy."

Yeah. Whatever.

But here's the thing: No matter what I say, it's not going to affect your decision, is it? Because you've already decided. And here's another thing: I can't seriously talk to you about being a soldier until you are one. Or are not one. Either of those people, I can talk to. I can say exactly what I think to either of those people. But to that third person, that might-end-up-being-a-soldier-but-might-not person? No, I've got nothing to say to you.

I joined the army because my daughter needed an operation. True story. I was twenty when I decided. My daughter needed an operation on one of her kidneys, a $30,000 operation, and we had no health insurance. The army has 100-percent health coverage for the whole family. Easy decision. I joined the army.

Here's another one: I joined the army because I had something to prove. True story. I was twenty, had very little self-confidence, and came to a point in my life where I realized—unconsciously, but it was there—that if I didn't do something really big and really hard to prove my self-worth to myself, I would likely end up a deflated wreck of a human being. I had a couple of ghosts to kill—high among them, the stepfather who'd humiliated and belittled me for close to twenty years—and it looked like the army might teach me how to kill those ghosts.

OK, those were two stories on why I joined the army. Both true stories. One hundred percent. Need me to go on? I could. I've got a million of 'em. All true.

How about you? What are the reasons racing around in your brain? What's up there in the front? And what's buried deep in the back?

Be honest.

Anyone who answers "saving the world for democracy" or "defending freedom" or "the war on terrorism" gets smacked in the back of the head. Smacked hard. Maybe twice. If you joined after 9/11 to go kick the ass of the people who killed my New York neighbors, I'm with you. But that's not where we're at, is it? We're in Iraq. Here are a few facts: Saddam Hussein had nothing to do with 9/11, period. And the presence of American soldiers in Iraq is making the world a more dangerous place for everyone, including Americans. If you didn't know those two facts, you're stupid and I don't want you in my army.

If you *do* know those two facts and you're still seriously thinking about joining . . . well, isn't that interesting. Now you've got my attention.

Because I didn't say those things to convince you not to join. I just wanted to make sure you knew them.

A few more: Someone died in Vietnam so our current president wouldn't have to go to war—there was a list of names, names of the young men who qualified for exemption, and someone got kicked off that list so our current president could be illegally put on it. You know that, right? Dan Rather and Rush Limbaugh and all the differing forces of media aside, everyone knows the truth. You do, too, right?

The current president—that's the same guy who won't go to the funerals of soldiers now. You know that, right?

His right-hand man, the current vice president, got five draft deferments but later went on to become CEO of a company that makes its profits off the Iraq War. You're completely aware of this?

I just need to know that you know.

Speaking of profiting from war, do you know who makes the equipment you'll use if you join the army? Do you know who makes the rifles and ammo and helmets? One of my drill sergeants said it best: "The lowest bidder."

I just need to know that you know.

Funny, I don't see your hand wavering at all. I don't see you arguing with my points above. You can't argue with what everyone knows, but I don't see your hand really wavering, either.

Because you've already made up your mind, haven't you?

The battlefields of history are strewn with the bodies of young men and women who died for their country. Or thought they did.

I don't want you to die for our country. I don't want you to die for George W. Bush, either. I don't want you to die—you're beautiful, do you know that? I don't want you in pain; I don't want you silenced. Motherfucker, look at me when I'm talking to you.

But you already know what it is you're going to do. And in the end, I don't need your reasons— the obvious ones or the buried-deep ones. Make sure *you* know the reasons, though. It'll make it easier to accomplish what you need to accomplish.

Make sure you know the truth of the world, and the reality of your place in it.

You're going to have to forget all of it when you go—the truth and what you think about the truth. If you don't push it aside, it will get in your way, and that's dangerous. Dangerous to yourself, and dangerous to your fellow soldiers. But the truth will live inside of you somewhere, a small light, and be your compass. (And man, we can use a few compasses right now.) The truth will sleep inside you, and it will be there for you later when you need it. Not if you get killed, of course. Nothing can help you then. But when—and oh please, I hope so—you come back. When you come back, there will be pieces of you missing. Maybe something big like a limb, maybe your sense of humor. Maybe something smaller, hopefully. There will be something gained, too, no question, if you come back. But something will be missing. And when you take off the uniform finally and reconcile it all, you're going to make yourself accountable. You're going to want to know why you lost whatever it is that's missing. And you better be able to give a good reason—and it better be *your* reason. Not George Bush's reason, not your recruiter's reason, not NBC News's reason, not your high-school gym teacher's reason.

If there's any truth to the phrase "defending freedom," it's simply that—more than you can imagine now—the truth will set you free.

I have no advice to give on what you should or should not do because you won't listen to my advice anyway. I certainly wouldn't have back when I was consciously and unconsciously deciding what to do.

I was pumping gas at an Exxon on Route 22 in New Jersey when I joined the army in 1991. My boss—a bearded horse trainer who made ends meet by running the night shift at this gas station—had been a paratrooper in Vietnam. For months I heard horror stories from him. Literal horror stories. Finally, as I was approaching my own decision (no, that's bullshit—the decision had been made), I asked him, "Forget about the draft—if you had to do it again, would you?"

He surprised me with his answer: "Yep."

"Why?" I said. After all that he'd told me, I couldn't figure it. "Why?"

"None of your damn business," he said. "The real question is: do you know why you're joining?"

"Yeah," I said.

"You sure you know?"

"Yeah."

"Why?"

"None of your damn business," I said.

"Well, then," he said. "There it is."

THE RECRUITMENT MINEFIELD

by Bill Bigelow

Bill Bigelow taught high-school social studies for almost thirty years and is an editor of Rethinking Schools *magazine, which first published a longer version of this piece. In January 2006 the* Harvard Law Review *carried a detailed article taking issue with the decision of the Ninth Circuit Court of Appeals in the Emiliano Santiago case that Bigelow discusses here.*

Emiliano Santiago.

Not many people know his name. But they should. Santiago joined the Oregon Army National Guard on June 28, 1996, shortly after his high-school graduation in Hermiston, Oregon. He served honorably, became a sergeant, and was discharged in June 2004, after eight years in the Guard.

But in October 2004, more than three months *after* his discharge, the government extended Santiago's termination date—to December 24, 2031. Yes, 2031; it's not a misprint. Santiago's unit was ordered to report on January 2, 2005, to Fort Sill, Oklahoma, where it would join other soldiers being sent to Afghanistan.

In November, Santiago's attorney, Steven Goldberg of the National Lawyers Guild, filed suit in federal court in Portland, arguing that the military had no right to order Santiago to active duty months after he'd been discharged. During Santiago's hearing in December, Matthew Lepore, the Justice Department attorney, agreed that Santiago's activation had come after his discharge. But Lepore said that because commanders of Santiago's unit had been told earlier that under the military's stop-loss policy, his unit *might* be mobilized, that was notification enough.

True, Lepore acknowledged, Santiago himself was never notified, but that made no difference. Lepore argued that the court was obliged to view this case through a "deferential lens"—to assume the military knew what was best for the military. Judge Owen M. Panner agreed. He ruled against Santiago, saying he believed that the military would be harmed more than Santiago if the court ruled against the government. Goldberg appealed to the Ninth Circuit Court of Appeals. *[The court ruled against Santiago. His case then went to the U.S. Supreme Court, which declined to hear it. Later he was deployed to Afghanistan to serve until the army chose to release him.—eds.]*

High-school teachers, counselors, students, and parents everywhere should know about Santiago's case. Think you're signing up for four years, or eight years? Think again. Santiago was nineteen when he entered the military. When his new discharge date rolls around, he'll be fifty-four—if the military doesn't extend it again.

Thanks to a provision in the No Child Left Behind legislation, military recruiters have easy access to high-school students these days. In Portland, where I teach, the school board in 1995 banned organizations that discriminate based on race, sex, or sexual orientation—including the U.S. military—from recruiting in the schools. NCLB overturned that ban, requiring that recruiters have "the same access to secondary school students as is provided generally to post-secondary educational institutions or to prospective employers of those students." The law also requires high schools to provide the military access to students' names, addresses, and telephone numbers—unless a parent or student contacts the school to deny permission to release this information.

It was against the backdrop of the Santiago ruling and increased recruiter access to students that Julie O'Neill, a teacher at Franklin High School, in Portland, Oregon, began a short unit on military recruitment with her senior political science students. Since I was on leave from teaching that year, Julie invited me to collaborate on the unit.

We began by asking students to write about their experiences with military recruiters. I was astounded by students' stories. One hundred percent of O'Neill's students—three untracked classes of almost forty students each—had been recruited in some manner by one or another branch of the military. Julie's students were typical of the high school as a whole: largely white and working class, with a relatively small number of Asian Americans, Latinos, African Americans, and Native Americans. Recruiters had come into classes ranging from Foods ("You have to be in the military to cook for the president, ya know" they claimed), to Oceanography, to Band, to Weight Training. Recruiters had visited the Latino Club, played a key role in the annual Field Day activities, worked with the student program that links seniors and freshmen, and approached students in the halls.

They'd badgered students in malls, called them repeatedly, e-mailed them, visited them at home, bought them school supplies, driven them around town, mailed them videos and DVDs, and invited them to mini-boot-camp weekends. Even students whose parents had asked the school in writing not to share information with recruiters reported being contacted multiple times. The recruiters' techniques were consistent: find out students' after-graduation aspirations and attempt to convince them that the military was the way to realize their goals.

I read all one-hundred-plus recruitment stories. The more I read, the more overwhelmed I became by the sense that today's students live in a kind of parallel universe where they maneuver daily through a psychological minefield of quota-driven recruiters.

And there was another pattern. Recruiters lie. One girl went with a friend to the recruitment office to take a math test. "When she was done with her test, he told us about how the government pays for you to go to college and after you serve, you still get money. I think that was the main reason my friend wanted to join—that and they told her that she wouldn't have to go to Iraq. How do they know?"

They don't; it was a lie. In a valuable article, "AWOL in America," in the March 2005 issue of *Harper's,* Kathy Dobie reports that the G.I. Rights Hotline has "heard hundreds of stories involving recruiters' lies." As Dobie reports, "One of the most common lies told by recruiters is that it's easy to get out of the military if you change your mind. But once they arrive at training, the recruits are told there's no exit, period—and if you try to leave, you'll be court-martialed and serve ten years in the brig; you'll never be able to get a good job or a bank loan, and this will follow you around like a felony conviction." It's not true, but as Dobie speculates, the threats are likely effective in keeping some unhappy soldiers from trying to get out. In fact, the expectation that recruiters make promises they can't back up is acknowledged in the enlistment contract that prospective soldiers must sign when entering the military.

It took me weeks to locate a copy of this enlistment contract. *[See http://www.rethinking schools.org/archive/19_03/military_enlistment.pdf]* Recruiters don't let prospects take it home; they don't let teachers have copies; they don't let parents have copies. No wonder. It's a scary document. Ask Emiliano Santiago.

For some young people, this document will be the most important contract they sign in their entire lives. Joining the military is a life-altering decision, and one that the government urges—indeed bullies—young people to make before they're deemed mature enough even to buy a bottle of beer. A critical examination of this document should be part of the core curriculum in every high school in the United States. It's not hyperbole to say that this study is a matter of life and death.

The "Enlistment/Reenlistment Document— Armed Forces of the United States"—its official title—is anything but straightforward. Section 8c implicitly acknowledges that some recruiters may have made false promises—as in the case of the girl who was told that she wouldn't be sent to Iraq. It reads: "The agreements in this section and attached annex(es) are all the promises made to me by the Government. ANYTHING ELSE ANYONE HAS PROMISED ME IS NOT VALID

AND WILL NOT BE HONORED" [emphasis in original].

Section 9 tells recruits: "Many laws, regulations, and military customs will govern my conduct and require me to do things a civilian does not have to do." The section states that a recruit will be subject to laws "which I cannot change but which Congress can change at any time." Reading this section prompted one student to ask, "How can one sign a contract that is always changing?"

Arguably the most important part of the contract is section 9b. It makes *all* promises in the document irrelevant:

> Laws and regulations that govern military personnel may change without notice to me. Such changes may affect my status, pay, allowances, benefits, and responsibilities as a member of the Armed Forces REGARDLESS of the provisions of this enlistment/reenlistment document [emphasis in original].

Congress must pass laws, but regulations are military matters, and changes in these could nullify other parts of the document. One student said, "Anything they promise you is BS. Look at it." Another added, "All this needs to say is, 'You're the military's. Sign there.'" Another wondered,

"How can the army focus so much on honor but not agree to honor agreements?"

We wanted students to understand the government's argument in the Santiago case, as it's a position that anyone considering enlistment should be aware of. Steven Goldberg had faxed us a part of the U.S. government's brief defending its cancellation of Santiago's discharge. It is grounded in the government's interpretation of the "contract" between the government and an enlistee. Here's a key passage from the brief filed with the Ninth Circuit Court of Appeals:

> Enlistment in the armed forces does not constitute merely a bargain between two parties, but effects a change of status by which "the citizen becomes a soldier": "no breach of the contract destroys the new status or relieves . . . the obligations which its existence imposes." *Bell v. United States, 366 U.S. 303, 402 (1961) (quoting in re Grimley, 17 U.S. 147, 151–152 (1890))*

In other words, it doesn't make any difference if the government violated the enlistment agreement with Santiago regarding his date of release from military service. Once he signed that contract, he was no longer merely a citizen but a soldier, and when you're a soldier, you're subject to military rule and laws governing the military.

During their senior year of high school, students can expect to be massively assaulted by military propaganda. Much is dishonest; much is manipulative. Helping them develop the capacity to question recruitment materials could literally save someone's life. If we don't help young people nurture this skeptical sensibility about military recruitment and enlistment, then our hidden agenda is "Do as you're told," "Trust the authorities," "The government knows best." This is profoundly undemocratic. It's a curriculum of ignorance. How we teach about vital issues like recruitment says something about the kind of world we want to help create. Do we want people to be active, questioning, and engaged, or simply to be consumers of other people's plans?

In a recent segment of PBS's *News Hour with Jim Lehrer,* Emiliano Santiago's mother said that as a high-school junior, Santiago had been "lured by the uniform of the recruiters." How students react to the lure of the uniform or any other recruitment ploy depends, in part, on whether they have been taught to think critically. As military authorities find it increasingly difficult to convince youngsters to enlist, they have begun to send even more recruiters into the field and to authorize larger payments to those who will sign up. Students need to realistically evaluate the hard sell and the lavish promises.

Editor's Note: Readers concerned about how the military goes about recruiting young people should know about No Child Left Unrecruited, *a documentary film made by two high-school students in Lawrence, Kansas. Sarah Ybarra and Alexia Welch's film has appeared on YouTube and been screened before members of Congress. The film aims to alert young people to tactics used by recruiters, including personal information that schools are pressured into releasing to the military. However, I believe that correcting abuses in recruitment is, at best, half of the problem. As long as we have a volunteer army, the military will do whatever it can to fill its quotas. I feel that until there is some form of national service that all teenagers are required to do—whether by helping to house and clothe the poor, to clean up the environment, to aid and comfort the ill or elderly, or to serve in the armed forces—we will live in a nation poisoned by the gap between those who (for whatever reason) serve and those who do not.—MA*

THE MOMENT OF COMBAT

by Chris Hedges

Chris Hedges spent nearly twenty years as a foreign correspondent for the New York Times *and other prominent newspapers, as well as for National Public Radio; he has reported from more than fifty nations around the world, often during times of war. In 2002 he was a member of a team of reporters that earned a Pulitzer Prize for its pieces explaining global terrorism. He holds a graduate degree from Harvard Divinity School and is a visiting lecturer at Princeton University. Every reader of this anthology should know his books,* War Is a Force That Gives Us Meaning *and* What Every Person Should Know About War. *In* What Every Person Should Know About War, *Chris used his skill as a reporter to gather the best information from experts about combat. An excerpt from that book follows this introduction.*

INTRODUCTION

I have spent most of my adult life in war. I began two decades ago covering wars in Central America, where I spent five years, then the Middle East, where I spent seven, and the Balkans, where I covered the wars in Bosnia and Kosovo. My life has been marred, let me say deformed, by the organized industrial violence that year after year was an intimate part of my existence. I have watched young men bleed to death on lonely Central

American dirt roads and cobblestoned squares in Sarajevo. I have looked into the eyes of mothers kneeling over the lifeless and mutilated bodies of their children. I have stood in warehouses with rows of corpses, including children, and breathed death into my lungs. I carry within me the ghosts of those I worked with, my comrades, now gone.

I have felt the attraction of violence. I know its seductiveness, excitement, and the powerful addictive narcotic it can become. The young soldiers, trained well enough to be disciplined but encouraged to maintain their naive adolescent belief in invulnerability, have in wartime more power at their fingertips than they will ever have again. They catapult from being minimum-wage employees at places like Burger King, facing a life of dead-end jobs with little hope of health insurance or adequate benefits, to being part of, in the words of the marines, "the greatest fighting force on the face of the earth." The disparity between what they were and what they have become is breathtaking and intoxicating. This intoxication is only heightened in wartime when all taboos are broken. Murder goes unpunished and often rewarded. The thrill of destruction fills their days with wild adrenaline highs, strange grotesque landscapes that are hallucinogenic, all accompanied by a sense of purpose and comradeship. These sights and emotions replace the alienation many left behind. They become accustomed to killing, carrying out acts of slaughter with no more forethought than they take to relieve themselves. The abuses committed against the helpless prisoners in Abu Ghraib or Guantánamo are not aberrations but the real face of war.

In wartime all human beings become objects, objects either to gratify or destroy or both. And almost no one is immune. The contagion of the crowd sees to that. "Force," Simone Weil wrote, "is as pitiless to the man who possesses it, or thinks he does, as it is to its victims. The second it crushes; the first it intoxicates."

This myth, the lie, about war, about ourselves, is imploding our democracy. We shun introspection and self-criticism. We ignore truth, to embrace the strange, disquieting certitude and hubris offered by the radical Christian Right. These radical Christians peddle a vision of Christ as the head of a great and murderous army of heavenly avengers, drawing almost exclusively from the book of Revelation, the only place in the Bible where Jesus sanctions violence. They rarely speak about Christ's message of love, forgiveness, and compassion. They relish the cataclysmic destruction that will befall unbelievers, including those such as myself, whom they dismiss as "nominal Christians." They divide the world between good and evil, between those anointed to act as agents of God and those who act as agents of Satan. The cult of masculinity and esthetic of violence pervades their ideology. Feminism and homosexuality are forces, believers are told, that have rendered the American male physically and spiritually impotent. Jesus, for the Christian Right, is a man of action, casting out demons, battling the Antichrist, attacking hypocrites, and castigating the corrupt. The language is one not only of exclusion, hatred, and fear, but a call for apocalyptic violence, in short the language of war.

In war, we always deform ourselves, our essence. We give up individual conscience—maybe even consciousness—for the contagion of the crowd, the rush of patriotism, the belief that we must stand together as a nation in moments of extremity. To make a moral choice, to defy war's enticement, to find moral courage, can be self-destructive.

The attacks on the World Trade Center illustrate that those who oppose us, rather than coming from another moral universe, have been schooled well in modern warfare. The dramatic explosions, the fireballs, the victims plummeting to their deaths, the collapse of the towers in Manhattan, were straight out of Hollywood. Where else but from the industrialized world did the suicide bombers learn that huge explosions and death above a city skyline are a peculiar and effective form of communication? They have mastered the language we have taught them. They understand that the use of indiscriminate violence against innocents is a way to make a statement. We leave the same calling cards. We delivered such incendiary messages in Vietnam, Serbia, Afghanistan, and Iraq. It was Secretary of Defense Robert McNamara who in the summer of 1965 defined the bombing raids that would kill hundreds of thousands of civilians north of Saigon as a means of communication to the Communist regime in Hanoi.

The most powerful antiwar testaments, evidence of what war is and what war does to us, appear outside of the battlefield. It is the suffering of the veterans whose body and mind are changed forever because they served a nation that sacrificed them, the suffering of families and children caught up in the unforgiving maw of war, which begin to tell the story of war. But we are not allowed to see dead bodies, at least not of our own soldiers, nor do we see the wounds that forever mark a life, the wounds that leave faces and bodies horribly disfigured by burns or shrapnel. We never watch the agony of the dying. War is made palatable. It is sanitized. We are allowed to taste war's perverse thrill but spared from seeing war's consequences. The wounded and the dead are swiftly carted offstage. And for this I blame the press, which willingly hides from us the effects of bullets, roadside bombs, and rocket-propelled grenades, which sat at the feet of those who lied to make this war possible and dutifully reported these lies and called it journalism.

War is always about this betrayal. It is about the betrayal of the young by the old, idealists by cynics and finally soldiers by politicians. Those who pay the price, those who are maimed forever by war, however, are crumpled up and thrown away. We do not see them. We do not hear them. They are doomed, like wandering spirits, to float around the edges of our consciousness, ignored, even reviled. The message they bring is too painful for us to hear. We prefer the myth of war, the myth of glory, honor, patriotism, and heroism, words that in the terror and brutality of combat are empty, meaningless, and obscene.

We are losing the war in Iraq. We are an isolated and reviled nation. We are pitiless to others weaker than ourselves. We have lost sight of our democratic ideals. Thucydides wrote of Athens's expanding empire and how this empire led it to become a tyrant abroad and then a tyrant at home. The tyranny Athens imposed on others, it finally imposed on itself. If we do not confront the lies and hubris told to justify the killing and mask the destruction carried out in our name in Iraq, if we do not grasp the moral corrosiveness of empire and occupation, if we continue to allow force and violence to be our primary form of communication, if we do not remove from power our flag-waving, cross-bearing versions of the Taliban, we will not so much defeat dictators such as Saddam Hussein as become them.

WAR IS...

An Excerpt from *What Every Person Should Know About War*

How will my body react to combat?

Your brain will activate its "fight or flight" system. It will release a massive discharge of stress hormones. Your heart rate will jump roughly from 70 beats per minute to more than 200 beats per minute in less than a second. Blood flow to your large muscle masses will increase, making you stronger and faster. Minor blood vessels in your hands and feet will constrict, to reduce bleeding from wounds. Some common by-products of this reaction are tunnel vision, the loss of fine and complex motor control, and the inability to think clearly. If you are confronted with sudden danger you may not know how to react. You may not be able to see, think, or control your body. During the first experience of combat you may have a shaking fit or curl up in the fetal position. You will probably recover within a few days.[1]

How will I perform during my first time in combat?

Your performance may be poor. It will be hard for you to adjust, identify, and respond to dangers such as incoming artillery. You have a relatively high risk of being wounded or killed in your first battle.[2]

Will I get better?

Almost definitely. Once you get over your initial nervousness your combat skills will improve. You will learn to evaluate threats and quickly react to hostile movements and sounds. Over time you will learn to face battle calmly. If your unit suffers heavy casualties, or the chance of surviving a long war seems poor, your skills may decline.[3]

Will I fire my weapon?

Probably, although this was not always the case. Less than half the riflemen in World War II and 55 percent in the Korean War fired their weapons. U.S. military training has become more adept at conditioning you to shoot. Ninety percent of front-line personnel fired their weapons in Vietnam.[4]

What will make me fire?

You will fire based on commands from your leader, enemy contact, or the sudden appearance of a target. The farther away you are from the enemy the easier it will be to pull the trigger. At close range, or in hand-to-hand combat, you will see the enemy as another human being and it will be harder to kill.[5]

Will it feel like training?

In some ways. In addition to fire and defense

skills, you will receive stress inoculation training. The military attempts to replicate the
noise, light, and intensity of combat. With
enough training, war may feel like another ex-
ercise. As one Ranger recalled about Somalia,
"I just started picking them out as they were
running across the intersection two blocks
away, and it was weird because it was so much
easier than you would think. It was so much
like basic training, they were just targets out
there, and I don't know if it was the training
that we had ingrained in us, but it seemed to
me it was just like watching a moving target
range and you could just hit the target and
watch it all and it wasn't real."[6]

Will it feel like a video game?

It might. Since the 1980s the military has used
video games for training. Games such as Doom,
Battlezone, and Microsoft Flight Simulator
have been adapted to introduce soldiers and
Marines to combat. The Marines are develop-
ing at least one military tool with a six-button
controller based on the console for the Sony
PlayStation because many recruits are very
familiar with the device.[7]

How can I avoid being shot by the enemy?

Avoid being seen. Rely on camouflage, physical defenses, and the cover of darkness. Stay

low to the ground. Try not to stay up longer than three to five seconds so the enemy cannot track you. Minimize movement. Put tape around your dog tags so they do not make noise. Avoid wearing jewelry or using tape that can reflect sunlight. Use greasepaint to cover skin oils. Exposed skin, even dark skin, reflects light.[8]

How should I prepare for battle?

Get some sleep, eat, clean your weapon, and review your mission. The most motivated personnel are the most likely to ignore their need for food, water, and rest.[9]

Will I get used to combat?

Maybe. Some combat veterans develop a high tolerance for battlefield stress and fight calmly. You may experience anxiety afterward, however, as you look back at the fight and review close calls.[10]

What does it feel like to kill someone?

You will probably go though several emotional reactions when you kill. These are generally sequential, but not necessarily universal. The first phase is concern that you'll freeze up and won't be able to pull the trigger. The second is the actual kill, which, because of your training, will happen reflexively. You may feel exhilarated. Killing produces adrenaline; repeated killing can lead to "killing addiction." This feeling can be especially intense if you kill at medium to long-range distances. The next phase, remorse and revulsion, can render you unable to ever kill again. [Lieutenant Colonel] Dave Grossman [Retired, US Army] presents this "collage of pain and horror": ". . . my experience was one of revulsion and disgust . . . I dropped my weapon and cried . . . there was so much blood . . . I vomited . . . and I cried . . . I felt remorse and shame . . . I can remember whispering foolishly, 'I'm sorry' and then just throwing up." Only a few people are able to kill and not feel remorse, though many try to deny this feeling to make it easier to continue to kill. Subsequent killings are often easier to handle. Last is the rationalization and acceptance phase. This is a lifelong process during which you will try to account for what you did. Most are able to see what they did as the right and necessary thing. If you cannot rationalize your killing it may lead to post-traumatic stress disorder.[11]

Will I feel guilty killing in combat?
Most likely. After the exhilaration of killing, you will probably experience a feeling of remorse. This may be accompanied by thoughts that you are "sick" or "wrong" for having

enjoyed killing. You may also have a profound feeling of responsibility for the dead—both comrades and enemies. Trying to reconcile this feeling of accountability will add more guilt. You may become agitated, angry, or withdrawn. In the Gulf War, stress and guilt from killing enemy soldiers was reduced somewhat because much of the killing was done from long distances. Using group-fired weapons allows individuals to feel less responsible for enemy deaths. Military training seeks to depersonalize the enemy, making it easier for you to kill without guilt. Veteran officer J. Glenn Gray wrote: "Professional officers consider part of the psychological training of their troops to be training in hatred, and this becomes more systemized and subtler as the war goes on."[12]

Will I feel worse if I kill an enemy in an ambush?
You may. Those who kill in an ambush often find the experience disturbing. Many say it is hard to watch someone die. It is also hard to look at documents, letters, and photographs of loved ones on the bodies of someone you have killed.[13]

Is it easier to bear killing an enemy you cannot see?
Yes. The most traumatic reactions come from attacking someone you can clearly identify as a human being.[14]

Is there a chance I will enjoy killing?

Yes. Some people enjoy killing. Even those who do not can find it exciting. Vietnam veteran R. B. Anderson discussed the thrill of killing in combat in his essay "Vietnam Was Fun (?)": "It was fun . . . it was great fun. In combat I was a respected man among men. I lived on life's edge and did the most manly thing in the world: I was a warrior in war . . . Only a veteran can know about the thrill of the kill." Some people get stuck in the exhilaration phase of killing, which means that they are able to kill over and over without remorse. This is especially true for snipers and pilots, whose killing is made easier by greater distance. Only about 2 percent of the population (3 to 4 percent of men and 1 percent of women) are considered "natural killers." This 2 percent typically accounts for up to 50 percent of the killing by a unit. The other 98 percent must overcome a natural resistance to killing. The intoxication of battle, however, can make killing attractive, even to those who do not at first find killing pleasant. J. Glenn Gray wrote: "Most men would never admit that they enjoyed killing, and there are a great many who do not. On the other hand, thousands of youth who never suspected the presence of such an impulse in themselves have learned in military life the mad excitement of destroying.[15]

Will I have to kill an enemy with my bare hands?

Probably not, though you will be trained to do so.[16]

What will it be like to see dead bodies?

You may be struck by how similar the combatants are to you in age and appearance. You may be disgusted by the appearance and smell of the decaying flesh.[17]

How will I react to the enemy dead?

You may be full of rage and want to exact revenge from the corpses by violating the bodies. The impulse can be strong. Collecting scalps, ears, gold teeth, and other body parts as trophies is common when there is a strong hatred toward an enemy. Leaving deliberately mutilated bodies (especially with facial and genital mutilation) for the enemy to find is less common, but also occurs. You may also take pictures of yourself and your comrades next to the enemy's dead bodies.[18]

Will I be afraid?

Yes. Fear affects everyone in combat. You may fear dying. You may fear being afraid in front of your comrades. You may fear unknown weapons. You may fear causing grief to your family if you die.[19]

What will happen to my body if I'm afraid?

In one division that saw heavy fighting in World War II, a quarter of the soldiers said they had been so scared during battle they vomited. A similar number said they had urinated or defecated in their pants during combat. This is a physical reaction to fear. It has nothing to do with your ability or willingness to fight.[20]

NOTES

1. U.S. Army Field Manual 6-22.5, "Combat Stress" (Washington, D.C.: 23 June 2000), secs. 1–4; Dave Grossman, *On Killing: The Psychological Cost of Learning to Kill in War and Society* (Boston: Little, Brown, 1996).

2. U.S. Army Field Manual 22-51, "Leaders' Manual for Combat Stress Control" (Washington, D.C.: 29 September 1994), sec. 2–8.

3. U.S. Army Field Manual 22-51, sec. 2–8.

4. D. Keith Shurtleff, "The Effects of Technology on Our Humanity," *Parameters,* Summer 2002, 100–12.

5. D. Keith Shurtleff, "The Effects of Technology," 100–12.

6. Peter Kilner, "Military Leaders' Obligation to Justify Killing in War," *Military Review,* March–April 2002, 24–31; Erica Goode, "Treatment

and Training Help Reduce Stress of War," *New York Times,* 25 March 2003, F1.

7. Harold Kennedy, "Computer Games Liven Up Military Recruiting, Training," *National Defense Magazine,* November 2002; William Hamilton, Toymakers Study Troops, and Vice Versa," *New York Times,* 30 March 2003, I1.

8. U.S. Army Field Manual 20-3, "Camouflage, Concealment, and Decoys" (Washington, D.C.: 30 August 1999); U.S. Army Field Manual 21–75, "Combat Skills of the Soldier" (Washington, D.C.: 3 August 1984), ch. 1; U.S. Army STP 21-1-SMCT, "Soldier's Manual of Common Tasks, Skill Level 1" (Washington, D.C.: 1 October 1990).

9. U.S. Army Field Manual 3-7, "NBC Field Handbook" (Washington, D.C.: 29 September 1994).

10. U.S. Army Field Manual 22-51, sec. 2–8.

11. Joanna Bourke, *An Intimate History of Killing: Face-to-Face Killing in Twentieth-Century Warfare* (New York: Basic Books, 1999); Dave Grossman, *On Killing,* 231–40.

12. U.S. Army Field Manual 22-51, 2–7; Faris R. Kirkland, Ronald R. Halverson, and Paul D. Bliese, "Stress and Psychological Readiness in Post-Cold War Operations," *Parameters,* Summer 1996, 79–91; J. Glenn Gray, *The Warriors: Reflections on Men in Battle* (New York: Harcourt, Brace, 1959), 161; Dave Grossman, *On Killing,* 75, 243–5.

13. U.S. Army Field Manual 22-51.

14. Dave Grossman and Bruce K. Siddle, "Psychological Effects of Combat," in *Encyclopedia of Violence, Peace, and Conflict,* eds. Lester Kurtz and Jennifer Turpin (San Diego: Academic Press, 1999).

15. David S. Pierson, "Natural Killers: Turning the Tide of Battle," *Military Review,* May 1999; J. Glenn Gray, *The Warriors,* 52; Jack Thompson, "Hidden Enemies," *Soldier of Fortune,* October 1985, 21; R. B. Anderson, "Parting Shot: Vietnam Was Fun (?)," *Soldier of Fortune,* November 1988, 96; Dave Grossman, *On Killing,* 231–240.

16. U.S. Army Field Manual 22-51, ch. 3.

17. Joanna Bourke, *An Intimate History of Killing.*

18. U.S. Army Field Manual 22-51, sec. 4–6; Joanna Bourke, *An Intimate History of Killing.*

19. Evan Thomas, "Fear at the Front," *Newsweek,* 3 February 2003, 34.

20. Dave Grossman and Bruce K. Siddle, "Psychological Effects of Combat."

THOU SHALT NOT KILL

an interview with army chaplain Lyn Brown

Dr. Lyn Brown, an Army National Guard chaplain, first came to my attention when I heard him interviewed on National Public Radio's This American Life, *talking about his difficulties in counseling young soldiers who came to him troubled about the conflict between the biblical commandment "Thou shalt not kill" and their role as soldiers. The producer of the show, Alex Blumberg, put me in touch with Chaplain Brown, and we talked more about his role as a religious counselor to the military.*—PC

Patty Campbell: So how did you happen to get into the military?

Chaplain Brown: Actually, I was a librarian in a Bible college and a seminary, and they were in financial difficulties, so I needed a second job. One day some soldiers appeared here at the college looking for a chaplain. I found out I was still young enough to get in—at that time I was thirty-eight—so I joined the Army National Guard in Maryland. I'd been a pastor in the Seattle area, where I was a librarian. So I still kept my ordination, kept doing things as a member of the clergy, but only on a part-time basis. The chaplaincy is only one weekend a month; in summer, it's annual training. I've been doing it for seventeen years now.

PC: Just what does a chaplain do?

LB: Well, a chaplain serves as a staff officer for a commander, and he could be a commander over three or four hundred people all the way up to a thousand. The chaplain is there to advise the commander on moral issues, on religious issues. Primarily they make sure that religious support is provided for all the soldiers.

PC: And you do pastoral counseling, then?

LB: Yes, that probably takes the majority of my time. I see that a soldier has a problem, or I anticipate a problem, or the commander or the first sergeant says to me, "So-and-so has a problem; I think you might want to talk to him."

PC: Well, that brings me to a really tricky question. When I heard you speak on NPR, you talked about your difficulty with counseling young soldiers who come to you and say, "It says in the Bible, 'Thou shalt not kill.'" Can you talk a little bit about that?

LB: Sure. Usually soldiers came because they were concerned in two major ways. One was they were concerned about their own mortality. Especially if you're a soldier in Iraq, you just never know when you're going to get a roadside bomb, or a missile.

The other issue people were looking at was their families, wondering about the impact on their lives. They were concerned about "Am I doing something I shouldn't be doing? Should I be home taking care of my family?"

PC: But what about the prohibition against killing?

LB: Well, a lot of times this would be brought up because an individual would be having second thoughts. Young soldiers were coming to me and asking about being conscientious objectors. They had been in combat, and they didn't like what they saw. I had one soldier who lost a buddy, and he sat there with him and held his hand until he died. Here's a kid who's twenty years old.

PC: All of a sudden, he realized . . .

LB: Yeah. He was like—I don't want to be here. What can I do? He was thinking about the fact that he had a girlfriend back home and a baby on the way and wondering "What are the different ways that I can get out of this situation?" where, obviously, his life was on the line. He talked to me about his responsibility as the father of the baby that was coming and how he needed to take care of the baby and his girlfriend, and he brought up the matter of conscientious objector status.

So we walked through that, talked about what that meant. And he brought up that the commandment is "Thou shalt not kill" and why are we over here killing people? So I said, "Well, let's back up a little bit and get a context. After the Ten Commandments were given, there were battles that were ordered by God, the children of Israel fighting against the people who were trying to stop them from going to the Promised Land, or taking it over when they got there. Battles were fought.

Also, Jesus had interaction with soldiers. There was one centurion, an officer, who came because his slave was sick, and he believed that Jesus could heal him. Jesus said something to him about his faith being great, even though he wasn't Jewish. At the same time, he didn't say, "Stop being a soldier" or "Stop being involved."

PC: But he didn't tell the tax collector to stop being a tax collector, either.

LB: Right. People had to function in their jobs, and he didn't label some of these jobs as being sinful. And another thing—as I look at the epistles of Paul, the terminology he uses, the figure of speech is the uniform of a soldier. Ephesians 6 says, "Put on the whole armor of God"—implying that the articles that are put on are defensive, to protect you, not offensive, like a sword. So we went through that, and I just explained that actually "Thou shalt not kill" referred to taking someone's life, what we would refer to as murder.

PC: Do you know if the Hebrew word is different?

LB: Yes it is. In Deuteronomy you see a distinction made between intentionally murdering someone and accidentally causing the death of another person. Judges were sought out to decide if it was murder or manslaughter. Those who were convicted of murder were immeditely put to death and those who were found guilty of manslaughter were required to live the remainder of their lives within the walls of a "city of refuge" away from family and friends who were seeking revenge.

PC: What about that scene in the Garden of Gethsemane when one of Jesus's followers whacked off the ear of one of the guards, and Jesus reached out his hand and healed it?

LB: Especially in that context, Jesus had a goal in mind, he had a mission, and of course, Peter sometimes had a tendency to act first and think later.

PC: On a different tack, how can it be that young men enlist and don't realize that they may be asked to kill? Or that they may get killed?

LB: Well, I don't know—young men especially think they're invincible. And I think there's a tendency to see it like video games; all you have to do is reset it and you come back to life again or something. You know, even though video games are violent, it isn't real bloodshed; you don't have a buddy losing his life. You know it's a game. When you get to the real stuff, it's a shock. It blows your mind. "I can't believe I'm here." I've had that feeling, too, under fire: "What's happening?" It's like being in a dream.

PC: And at that point, evidently, some young soldiers come to you and start reexamining their feelings about the whole thing. Do you think it's because they're so young?

LB: Well, the other problem we have in this culture, too, is when soldiers—especially young soldiers—come back from Afghanistan or Iraq and they have a lot of money that has been saved up because they couldn't spend it while they were away. They go out and buy a motorcycle, drive crazy, and get killed. Lots of fatalities.

PC: What do you think is behind that?

LB: Well, it's invincibility. They don't think anything is going to happen to them.

PC: Because they've survived in Afghanistan or Iraq?

LB: Yes, but there just isn't any caution. They haven't had real life experience, and they can do something stupid way beyond what they really intend. You can't just push the reset button and start over.

PC: Do you, as a mature man of God, ever find yourself in conflict with the conduct of war?

LB: Uh—yeah. I see, on both sides, people in anger. Ultimately it's our political leaders who have to make the decisions to put us in harm's way. They don't put *themselves* in harm's way. They're the ones who call people up, but you know there's always the Cause. I saw that even with various Iraqis I talked to—everybody has their own arguments. I saw people killed and severely injured. My heart went out to countries where people are victims or families are affected. I would just hope that our leaders would really think hard about going to war, realize there are serious repercussions and serious consequences that they may not even know.

PC: Yes, some hard thinking needs to be done. You know, I'm always aware that Jesus told us to love our enemies, and yet how difficult that is in the modern world.

LB: Well, there's a lot of things that God tells us to do that are hard. It's harder than the natural way of doing things—self-control, turning the other cheek, sometimes allowing people to take advantage of you, not jumping back at them. . . .

PC: In the end, were you able to get the young man conscientious objector status?

LB: Actually, it ended up we didn't have to. He was trying to readjust, and we helped him deal with the trauma. We transferred him from going out every day and moved him to the headquarters area, where he didn't have to go out for a while. He was able to go home on R and R and come back, and he said, "Hey, I'm ready to go back out. My girlfriend talked to me about it and it's OK." So it turned out well. I was thankful that we had people who were in charge who were understanding and compassionate.

PC: So it would be possible to get conscientious objector status *after* you have enlisted?

LB: Yes, you can. But it's a very rare thing. You've got to look into a person's motives. Probably over the last seventeen years there were twelve people that I needed to interview for conscientious objector status, and I would say that the majority of them had some other ulterior motive. It wasn't a theological or philosophical or spiritual reason. They just wanted to see if they could avoid getting killed or even being deployed.

PC: Do you think we'll ever get over this business of waging war?

LB: Well, I think the only time we'll get over war is when God returns and establishes His government.

PC: The Kingdom of God, when the lion lies down with the lamb.

LB: Yes. That's the only way it's going to happen. I'm just thankful that God is in the equation.

Editor's Note: Chaplain Brown may have had in mind some of the many biblical foretellings of an endtime of peace, like this poetic passage by the prophet Isaiah in which he describes a world without war:

> They shall beat their swords into plowshares, and their spears into pruning hooks; nation shall not lift up sword against nation, neither shall they learn war any more.
>
> —Isaiah 2:4—PC

THE WAR PRAYER

by Mark Twain

Like Jon Stewart, Jay Leno, and Bill Maher today, Mark Twain drew on his enormous popularity as a humorist to comment on the events of the day. In 1904 he wrote this short story out of his anger at what he saw as America's imperialism in the Spanish-American War, but evidently the piece was too hot to handle. After Harper's Bazaar *rejected it as "not quite suited to a woman's magazine," Twain wrote a friend, "I don't think the prayer will be published in my time. None but the dead are permitted to tell the truth." The piece was found among his papers after he died, in 1910, but not until many years later was "The War Prayer" eventually printed. It has since become an antiwar classic.*

It was a time of great and exalting excitement. The country was up in arms, the war was on, in every breast burned the holy fire of patriotism; the drums were beating, the bands playing, the toy pistols popping, the bunched firecrackers hissing and spluttering; on every hand and far down the receding and fading spread of roofs and balconies a fluttering wilderness of flags flashed in the sun; daily the young volunteers marched down the wide avenue gay and fine in their new uniforms, the proud fathers and mothers and sisters and sweethearts cheering them with voices choked with happy emotion as they swung by; nightly the packed mass meetings listened, panting, to patriot oratory which stirred the deepest deeps of their hearts, and which they interrupted at briefest intervals with cyclones of applause, the tears running down their cheeks the while; in the churches the pastors preached devotion to flag and country, and invoked the God of Battles beseeching His aid in our good cause in outpourings of fervid eloquence which moved every listener. It was indeed a glad and gracious time, and the half dozen rash spirits that ventured to disapprove of the war and cast a doubt upon its righteousness straightway got such a stern and angry warning that for their personal safety's sake they quickly shrank out of sight and offended no more in that way.

Sunday morning came—next day the battalions would leave for the front; the church was filled; the volunteers were there, their young faces alight with martial dreams—visions of the stern advance, the gathering momentum, the rushing charge, the flashing sabers, the flight of the foe, the tumult, the enveloping smoke, the fierce pursuit, the surrender! Then home from the war, bronzed heroes, welcomed, adored, submerged in golden seas of glory! With the volunteers sat their dear ones, proud, happy, and envied by the neighbors and friends who had no sons and brothers to send forth to the field of honor, there to win for the flag, or, failing, die the noblest of noble deaths. The service proceeded; a war chapter from the Old Testament was read; the first prayer was said; it was followed by an organ burst that shook the building, and with one impulse the house rose, with glowing eyes and beating hearts, and poured out that tremendous invocation

> "God the all-terrible! Thou who ordainest!
> Thunder thy clarion and lightning thy sword!"

Then came the "long" prayer. None could remember the like of it for passionate pleading and moving and beautiful language. The burden of its supplication was, that an ever-merciful and benignant Father of us all would watch over our noble young soldiers, and aid, comfort, and encourage them in their patriotic work; bless them, shield them in the day of battle and the hour of peril, bear them in His mighty hand, make them strong and confident, invincible in the bloody onset; help them to crush the foe, grant to them and to their flag and country imperishable honor and glory—

An aged stranger entered and moved with slow and noiseless step up the main aisle, his eyes fixed upon the minister, his long body clothed in a robe that reached to his feet, his head bare, his white hair descending in a frothy cataract to his shoulders, his seamy face unnaturally pale, pale even to ghastliness. With all eyes following him and wondering, he made his silent way; without pausing, he ascended to the preacher's side and stood there waiting. With shut lids the preacher, unconscious of his presence, continued with his moving prayer, and at last finished it with the words, uttered in fervent appeal, "Bless our arms, grant us the victory, O Lord our God, Father and Protector of our land and flag!"

The stranger touched his arm, motioned him to step aside—which the startled minister did—and took his place. During some moments he surveyed the spellbound audience with solemn eyes, in which burned an uncanny light; then in a deep voice he said:

"I come from the Throne—bearing a message from Almighty God!" The words smote the house with a shock; if the stranger perceived it he gave no attention. "He has heard the prayer of His servant your shepherd, and will grant it if such shall be your desire after I, His messenger, shall have explained to you its import—that is to say, its full import. For it is like unto many of the prayers of men, in that it asks for more than he who utters it is aware of—except he pause and think.

"God's servant and yours has prayed his prayer. Has he paused and taken thought? Is it one prayer? No, it is two—one uttered, the other not. Both have reached the ear of Him Who heareth all supplications, the spoken and the unspoken. Ponder this—keep it in mind. If you would beseech a blessing upon yourself, beware! lest without intent you invoke a curse upon a neighbor at the same time. If you pray for the blessing of rain upon your crop which needs it, by that act you are possibly praying for a curse upon some neighbor's crop which may not need rain and can be injured by it.

"You have heard your servant's prayer—the uttered part of it. I am commissioned of God to put into words the other part of it—that part which the pastor—and also you in your hearts—fervently prayed silently. And ignorantly and unthinkingly? God grant that it was so! You heard these words: 'Grant us the victory, O Lord our God!' That is sufficient. The *whole* of the uttered prayer is compact into those pregnant words. Elaborations were not necessary. When you have prayed for victory you have prayed for many unmentioned results which follow victory—*must* follow it, cannot help but follow it. Upon the listening spirit of God fell also the unspoken part of the prayer. He commandeth me to put it into words. Listen!

"O Lord our Father, our young patriots, idols of our hearts, go forth to battle—be Thou near them! With them—in spirit—we also go forth from the sweet peace of our beloved firesides to smite the foe. O Lord our God, help us to tear their soldiers to bloody shreds with our shells; help us to cover their smiling fields with the pale forms of their patriot dead; help us to drown the thunder of the guns with the shrieks of their wounded, writhing in pain; help us to lay waste their humble homes with a hurricane of fire; help us to wring the hearts of their unoffending widows with unavailing grief; help us to turn them out roofless with little children to wander unfriended the wastes of their desolated land in rags and hunger and thirst, sports of the sun flames of summer and the icy winds of winter, broken in spirit, worn with travail, imploring Thee for the refuge of the grave and denied it—for our sakes who adore Thee, Lord, blast their hopes, blight their lives, protract their bitter pilgrimage, make heavy their steps, water their way with their tears, stain the white snow with the blood of their wounded feet! We ask it, in the spirit of love, of Him Who is the Source of Love, and Who is the ever-faithful refuge and friend of all that are sore beset and seek His aid with humble and contrite hearts. Amen.

[After a pause.] "Ye have prayed it; if ye still desire it, speak! The messenger of the Most High waits!"

It was believed afterward that the man was a lunatic, because there was no sense in what he said.

MASTERS OF WAR

a song by Bob Dylan

*The iconic sixties poet and folksinger Bob Dylan
speaks out about his vision of social justice in many
protest songs, such as "Blowin' in the Wind," which
have become part of the American consciousness.*

Come you masters of war
You that build all the guns
You that build the death planes
You that build the big bombs
You that hide behind walls
You that hide behind desks
I just want you to know
I can see through your masks

You that never done nothin'
But build to destroy
You play with my world
Like it's your little toy
You put a gun in my hand
And you hide from my eyes
And you turn and run farther
When the fast bullets fly

Like Judas of old
You lie and deceive
A world war can be won
You want me to believe

But I see through your eyes
And I see through your brain
Like I see through the water
That runs down my drain

You fasten the triggers
For the others to fire
Then you set back and watch
When the death count gets higher
You hide in your mansion
As young people's blood
Flows out of their bodies
And is buried in the mud

You've thrown the worst fear
That can ever be hurled
Fear to bring children
Into the world
For threatening my baby
Unborn and unnamed
You ain't worth the blood
That runs in your veins

How much do I know
To talk out of turn
You might say that I'm young
You might say I'm unlearned
But there's one thing I know
Though I'm younger than you

WAR IS...

Even Jesus would never
Forgive what you do

Let me ask you one question
Is your money that good
Will it buy you forgiveness
Do you think that it could
I think you will find
When your death takes its toll
All the money you made
Will never buy back your soul

And I hope that you die
And your death'll come soon
I will follow your casket
In the pale afternoon
And I'll watch while you're lowered
Down to your deathbed
And I'll stand o'er your grave
'Til I'm sure that you're dead

EXPERIENCING WAR

LETTERS FROM "OVER THERE," 1919

excerpts from the World War I letters of
Fred Duane Cowan

Many of the bright young boys of my father's generation, in a fervor of patriotism, rushed to enlist to fight World War I as soon as they turned eighteen. It is my guess that the two years my father spent in the marines was the peak experience of his life and that nothing afterward was nearly as exciting. For him it was a time of fun, of adventure, of getting to see places and people he would otherwise never have encountered. Although he endured physical hardship in the primitive conditions of military life on the move, he never had to take part in actual fighting because of the timing of his enlistment. He arrived in Europe just before Armistice Day in November 1918 and served in the American Army of Occupation in the uncertain time before the Treaty of Versailles and its sister treaties finally ended the war in 1919. In these fragments written to his parents and his sisters, Nell and Aurie, we see a naive and very young marine, untested in battle, innocently proud of his outfit, horsing around with his comrades, and bewildered and delighted by his encounters with European culture—a very different kind of experience from the disillusionment and suffering reflected in the more familiar writings about World War I.—PC

Paris, France
June 18, 1918

Dear Mother,

Well, at last we have left Germany and are in a civilized country again. We went up the Moselle River from Koblenz, passed about thirty miles north of Metz, went through Verdun and Châlons. The last place is quite a historic place, you know; that's where Attila the Hun was defeated and where he got on top of his plunder, set it on fire, and was burned to death.

Well, enough of history. I must tell you about Paris. I could write for an hour about it, and I spent one evening there. To start with, the Stadium camp is quite a ways from the heart of the city. I goes out to the car line and gets on a car city bound. A blue devil asked me for a cigarette (they sure are fond of American tobacco) and asked me where I was going. He suggested that I ought first to see the Boulevard De Italia and said he'd show me the way. We rode awhile on the car, then got on the subway and went to the Bastille and changed to another subway and went on to the Boulevard, where the Frenchman very politely shook hands, wished me a very *bon* time and shoved off.

The first thing I noticed was the number of pretty girls. Holy smokes. I'd see one coming that looked like a fashion magazine cover, and I'd say to myself, "There's just about as trim and neat and purty a little girl as ever went down the street," and then right behind her would come one that had her skinned a dozen different ways.

After strolling up and down awhile, I went into a café and got some ham and eggs, French fries, etc. The *garçon* didn't *compre* "ham and—" American style, for he brought two fried eggs and a side dish of *boiled ham*. I didn't say nothing cause the eggs themselves were a real treat.

After eating I went out and wandered around some more till it started to get dark and I thought I'd better make tracks for home. I found the station all right and after many adventures got the right train and arrived at the Bastille station. There I was stuck. I couldn't remember at what station I got on the other subway, therefore I didn't know where I wanted to go to. I was standing looking at a map trying to remember some of the stations I had come through, but I didn't see any familiar names at all. I guess I looked sort of lost cause an old gent come up and asked me in excellent English if he could help me in any way. He showed me how to get back to my camp and put me on the right train and told me where to get off at.

I got to the camp all right but my troubles had only begun. There are about 15,000 men here. Imagine going around in a city where the houses were all alike, and at eleven, and everybody you did meet were foreigners. Add to that the fact that the streets are not named and the houses not numbered, and you can see what a nice promenade I had.

I finally bumped into a French officer who couldn't tell where my company was, but he took me to his barracks and offered me a spare cot. I thanked him very profusely and was taking my leggings off when I heard 3 or 4 fellows arguing outside. Somebody kicked the door open and a voice says, "Hey, Frogs, where's the Americaine Regiment?" Such a chorus of *"Sacre's"* and *"Diablo's"* as followed. That's the trouble with the Americans. If you treat a frenchy decent and be exquisitely polite and say *pardon* and *merci* and *boo coo,* why, he'll do anything for you, while if you accost him in a belligerent or familiar way he gets insulted, and if he does give you any directions the chances are about 9 out of 10 that he will show you wrong just to get even.

Well, as I was saying, the Frogs were all sitting up in bed cussing the Americans for raising so much racket. The officer got up and expressing himself in the only two words of English he knew, he says *"Good night!"* and slams the door and goes back to bed, a-talking to himself.

I put on my leggins in a hurry and after saying good night to the Frenchies, beat it down the street and joined the other four Americans. We wandered around for about 15 minutes and by luck got into our own part of camp.

Now, those four fellows will tell you that the French soldiers don't like the Americans and won't even do the least thing to help them out. I don't know much about them as I spent very near all my time in Germany, but judging from what few incidents I have seen, the fault seems to be a little bit on the Americans' side, too.

With best of love,
Fred

Paris, France
July 1st, 1919

Dear Dad,

These be wild times here in gay Paree. The night of the June 28th, when peace was signed, everybody in Paris turned out to make it a big night, and believe me, they sure succeeded. The evening was opened by some big singer singing "The Marseillaise" from the balcony of the Opera. When she ended, things started with a whoop. I never saw such a crazy bunch of people in my life. Impromptu parades going up and down all the boulevards constantly. Firecrackers, skyrockets, confetti, paper streamers galore. Dances going on all the side streets. Soldiers of all nations were everywhere. Hats changed hands violently and often. I can still see a big lumbering Russian coming down the street with a big grin and a mademoiselle's hat perched on the side of his head. Behind him came an American with a shiny stovepipe hat. Somebody landed on it and it folded up like one of those hats you see on the stage.

At 3 A.M. I had enough. Things were still going as lively as ever when I left. Last night was the same thing over again.

Fred

Paris, France
July 27, 1919

Dear Dad,

The people in London treated us fine, as for a wonder the whole gang behaved themselves and acted in a very gentlemanly way. This bunch is the wildest gang I ever tied up with. In Germany when we were first organized the bunch had a reputation that traveled all over the sector. Every morning at sick call there was always a lineup to get treatment for black eyes, skinned knuckles, and sprained wrists, and there was always a dozen or more men from each company in the brig. The marines were the big toads in the puddle. There always has been hard feeling between the Third Division and the marines, and one day we went out on the ball field where the Third was playing ball. There were at least 5 or 6,000 of them, and our one company of 250 men invited the whole g— d— bunch to come down and fight. We not only asked but pleaded with them to come down out of the grandstand and settle our little differences. They sat like a bunch of wooden Indians and took all the names we could call them, but we got them in town that night and run 'em till their tongues hung out.

The poor colonel got prematurely grayheaded trying to keep some semblance of discipline. He would put the camp under restriction and the whole gang would go to town anyways and raise all kinds of h—.

The first couple weeks in Paris they tamed down some, and when we got to London they were a bunch of little lambs, with the exception of one night when a bunch of drunken Tommies got in under our windows at about 2 A.M. and started singing "Over There." If there is any song that will get a soldier's goat that was the one. I can't explain it, but it's the most detested song there is. We have had to stand at attention so many times and take it, while the sweat run down our legs and our feet would go to sleep and that hot iron helmet getting hotter and heavier all the time, while those d— bugles keep clamoring—Over there, over there, over there, over there, over there, over there. . . . That may have something to do with it, I don't know. Well, to realize what happened you must first grasp the tactical situation.

1. A three-story brick building on a corner. Lower floor: dining hall. Second floor and third floor: two big sleeping rooms, about 100 beds each.
2. Under every other bed—a pot.
3. Windows wide open every six feet.

Draw your own conclusions.

After the barrage lifted, there wasn't a Tommy in sight, and we had no more serenades all the time we were there.

I must tell you about the parade in

London. We left Paris on the morning of the 15th and went to Le Havre, getting there late at night, loaded into the transport at midnight, and sailed for England next morning. The channel was like a pond. Went to London by passenger coaches in an hour and a half. The same being the first cushions any of us had ridden on since leaving the States. Always before we rode in box cars, 42 men to a car. Why, honestly, it was so crowded at night that if the fellow in the middle of the car sneezed, the man on the end would bump his head against the end of the car.

We got off the train at Westminster station and marched to our billets, which were about a block from Westminster Abbey. The Abbey is a gloomy old stone church and has all the bones of England's dead kings and great people. I remember one which was something like "Cedric, King of the East Saxons, died 405." Sounds sort of romantic, don't it? All the same, I bet the old duffer used to pick his teeth at the table and wipe his greasy fingers on his breeches same as anybody. I didn't stay long because the place gave me the creeps.

The day before the big parade General Pershing and the Prince of Wales inspected the regiment in Hyde Park. The Prince of Wales is only about eighteen years old and is the regular conceited lime juicer type. He is undersized and puny. When he passed our squad, which are all nearly as tall as me—and I weigh almost 200 pounds now and none of the rest weigh under 180—he looked us up and down and says "Magnificent, ah-h, soldiers, General, eh what?" I was wondering all the time if he would go as high as the general's head if one of us would kick him in the seat of the pants.

The next day the big parade came off. The people went out to the line of march and camped all night so as to be sure and have a place. By daybreak the streets were packed. The papers say that over three million people viewed the parade in Paris on July 14. The London parade was twice as long but the streets were not as wide, so I suppose there were about the same number of people as in Paris. It took us three hours to make the route. We did eyes left and looked at the king and queen of England. She is a tall stately dame and looked more like a queen than Georgie looks like a king.

If you see a close-up of our company in the newsreels, you will know them by the star and Indian head painted on the front of the helmets.

We just got word that we are to return to the states about the third week in August and parade in New York and Washington. This is straight official dope.

Best of love to you and Ma,
Fred

P.S. If you come to New York to see the Parade bring a couple of those blackberry pies with you that you were talking about.

IN THE FRONT LINES

columns by Ernie Pyle

Ernie Pyle was a new kind of war reporter. He was not trying to capture the excitement of battle or to let folks back home know who was winning or why. He did not write about generals and campaigns; he wrote about men. He described the grunts, the foot soldiers, whom he walked with, slept beside, and knew as human beings. He mainly covered World War II in Europe—including the three pieces on the D-day landing we have included here. In fact, like many soldiers, he did not want to go on to the Pacific after Europe was won. But he did go, and it was near the island of Okinawa, on April 18, 1945, that he was killed. Pyle had won the Pulitzer Prize for his reporting, and his columns are still powerful today. One great place to start getting to know his work is http://www.journalism.indiana.edu/news/erniepyle/, where you can find and download many of his World War II articles.

THE GOD-DAMNED INFANTRY

IN THE FRONT LINES BEFORE MATEUR, NORTHERN TUNISIA, MAY 2, 1943—We're now with an infantry outfit that has battled ceaselessly for four days and nights.

This northern warfare has been in the mountains. You don't ride much anymore. It is walking and climbing and crawling country. The mountains aren't big, but they are constant. They are

WAR IS...

largely treeless. They are easy to defend and bitter to take. But we are taking them.

The Germans lie on the back slope of every ridge, deeply dug into foxholes. In front of them the fields and pastures are hideous with thousands of hidden mines. The forward slopes are left open, untenanted, and if the Americans tried to scale these slopes they would be murdered wholesale in an inferno of machine-gun crossfire plus mortars and grenades.

Consequently we don't do it that way. We have fallen back to the old warfare of first pulverizing the enemy with artillery, then sweeping around the ends of the hill with infantry and taking them from the sides and behind.

I've written before how the big guns crack and roar almost constantly throughout the day and night. They lay a screen ahead of our troops. By magnificent shooting they drop shells on the back slopes. By means of shells timed to burst in the air a few feet from the ground, they get the Germans even in their foxholes. Our troops have found that the Germans dig foxholes down and then under, trying to get cover from the shell bursts that shower death from above.

Our artillery has really been sensational. For once we have enough of something and at the right time. Officers tell me they actually have more guns than they know what to do with.

All the guns in any one sector can be centered to shoot at one spot. And when we lay the whole business on a German hill the whole slope seems to erupt. It becomes an unbelievable cauldron of fire and smoke and dirt. Veteran German soldiers say they have never been through anything like it.

Now to the infantry—the God-damned infantry, as they like to call themselves.

I love the infantry because they are the underdogs. They are the mud-rain-frost-and-wind boys. They have no comforts, and they even learn to live without the necessities. And in the end they are the guys that wars can't be won without.

I wish you could see just one of the ineradicable pictures I have in my mind today. In this particular picture I am sitting among clumps of sword-grass on a steep and rocky hillside that we have just taken. We are looking out over a vast rolling country to the rear.

A narrow path comes like a ribbon over a hill miles away, down a long slope, across a creek, up a slope and over another hill.

All along the length of this ribbon there is now a thin line of men. For four days and nights they have fought hard, eaten little, washed none, and slept hardly at all. Their nights have been violent with attack, fright, butchery, and their days sleepless and miserable with the crash of artillery.

The men are walking. They are fifty feet apart,

for dispersal. Their walk is slow, for they are dead weary, as you can tell even when looking at them from behind. Every line and sag of their bodies speaks their inhuman exhaustion.

On their shoulders and backs they carry heavy steel tripods, machine-gun barrels, leaden boxes of ammunition. Their feet seem to sink into the ground from the overload they are bearing.

They don't slouch. It is the terrible deliberation of each step that spells out their appalling tiredness. Their faces are black and unshaven. They are young men, but the grime and whiskers and exhaustion make them look middle-aged.

In their eyes as they pass is not hatred, not excitement, not despair, not the tonic of their victory—there is just the simple expression of being here as though they had been here doing this forever, and nothing else.

The line moves on, but it never ends. All afternoon men keep coming round the hill and vanishing eventually over the horizon. It is one long tired line of antlike men.

There is an agony in your heart and you almost feel ashamed to look at them. They are just guys from Broadway and Main Street, but you wouldn't remember them. They are too far away now. They are too tired. Their world can never be known to you, but if you could see them just once, just for an instant, you would know that no matter how hard people work back home they are not keeping pace with these infantrymen in Tunisia.

A PURE MIRACLE

NORMANDY BEACHHEAD, JUNE 12, 1944—
Due to a last-minute alteration in the arrangements, I didn't arrive on the beachhead until the morning after D-day, after our first wave of assault troops had hit the shore.

By the time we got here the beaches had been taken and the fighting had moved a couple of miles inland. All that remained on the beach was some sniping and artillery fire, and the occasional startling blast of a mine geysering brown sand into the air. That plus a gigantic and pitiful litter of wreckage along miles of shoreline.

Submerged tanks and overturned boats and burned trucks and shell-shattered jeeps and sad little personal belongings were strewn all over these bitter sands. That plus the bodies of soldiers lying in rows covered with blankets, the toes of their shoes sticking up in a line as though on drill. And other bodies, uncollected, still sprawling grotesquely in the sand or half hidden by the high grass beyond the beach.

That plus an intense, grim determination of work-weary men to get this chaotic beach organized and get all the vital supplies and the reinforcements moving more rapidly over it from the stacked-up ships standing in droves out to sea.

Now that it is over it seems to me a pure miracle that we ever took the beach at all. For some of our units it was easy, but in this special sector where I am now our troops faced such odds that our getting ashore was like my whipping Joe Louis down to a pulp.

In this column I want to tell you what the opening of the second front in this one sector entailed, so that you can know and appreciate and forever be humbly grateful to those both dead and alive who did it for you.

Ashore, facing us, were more enemy troops than we had in our assault waves. The advantages were all theirs, the disadvantages all ours. The Germans were dug into positions that they had been working on for months, although these were not yet all complete. A one-hundred-foot bluff a couple of hundred yards back from the beach had great concrete gun emplacements built right into the hilltop. These opened to the sides instead of to the front, thus making it very hard for naval fire from the sea to reach them. They could shoot parallel with the beach and cover every foot of it for miles with artillery fire.

Then they had hidden machine-gun nests on the forward slopes, with crossfire taking in every inch of the beach. These nests were connected by networks of trenches, so that the German gunners could move about without exposing themselves.

Throughout the length of the beach, running zigzag a couple of hundred yards back from the shoreline, was an immense V-shaped ditch fifteen feet deep. Nothing could cross it, not even men on foot, until fills had been made. And in other places at the far end of the beach, where the ground is flatter, they had great concrete walls. These were blasted by our naval gunfire or by explosives set by hand after we got ashore.

Our only exits from the beach were several swales or valleys, each about one hundred yards wide. The Germans made the most of these funnel-like traps, sowing them with buried mines. They contained, also, barbed-wire entanglements with mines attached, hidden ditches, and machine guns firing from the slopes.

This is what was on the shore. But our men had to go through a maze nearly as deadly as this before they even got ashore. Underwater obstacles were terrific. The Germans had whole fields of evil devices under the water to catch our boats. Even now, several days after the landing, we have cleared only channels through them and cannot yet approach the whole length of the beach with our ships. Even now some ship or boat hits one of these mines every day and is knocked out of commission.

The Germans had masses of those great six-pronged spiders, made of railroad iron and standing shoulder-high, just beneath the surface of the water for our landing craft to run into. They also had huge logs buried in the sand, pointing upward and outward, their tops just below the water. Attached to these logs were mines.

In addition to these obstacles they had floating mines offshore, land mines buried in the sand of the beach, and more mines in checkerboard rows in the tall grass beyond the sand. And the enemy had four men on shore for every three men we had approaching the shore.

And yet we got on.

Beach landings are planned to a schedule that is set far ahead of time. They all have to be timed, in order for everything to mesh and for the following waves of troops to be standing off the beach and ready to land at the right moment.

As the landings are planned, some elements of the assault force are to break through quickly, push on inland, and attack the most obvious enemy strong points. It is usually the plan for units to be inland, attacking gun positions from behind, within a matter of minutes after the first men hit the beach.

I have always been amazed at the speed called for in these plans. You'll have schedules calling for engineers to land at H-hour plus two minutes, and service troops at H-hour plus thirty minutes, and even for press censors to land at H-hour plus seventy-five minutes. But in the attack on this special portion of the beach where I am—the worst we had, incidentally—the schedule didn't hold.

Our men simply could not get past the beach. They were pinned down right on the water's edge by an inhuman wall of fire from the bluff. Our first waves were on that beach for hours, instead of a few minutes, before they could begin working inland.

You can still see the foxholes they dug at the very edge of the water, in the sand and the small, jumbled rocks that form parts of the beach.

Medical corpsmen attended the wounded as best they could. Men were killed as they stepped out of landing craft. An officer whom I knew got a bullet through the head just as the door of his landing craft was let down. Some men were drowned.

The first crack in the beach defenses was finally accomplished by terrific and wonderful naval gunfire, which knocked out the big emplacements. They tell epic stories of destroyers that ran right up into shallow water and had it out point-blank with the big guns in those concrete emplacements ashore.

When the heavy fire stopped, our men were organized by their officers and pushed on inland, circling machine-gun nests and taking them from the rear.

As one officer said, the only way to take a beach

is to face it and keep going. It is costly at first, but it's the only way. If the men are pinned down on the beach, dug in and out of action, they might as well not be there at all. They hold up the waves behind them, and nothing is being gained.

Our men were pinned down for a while, but finally they stood up and went through, and so we took that beach and accomplished our landing. We did it with every advantage on the enemy's side and every disadvantage on ours. In the light of a couple of days of retrospection, we sit and talk and call it a miracle that our men ever got on at all or were able to stay on.

Before long it will be permitted to name the units that did it. Then you will know to whom this glory should go. They suffered casualties. And yet if you take the entire beachhead assault, including other units that had a much easier time, our total casualties in driving this wedge into the continent of Europe were remarkably low—only a fraction, in fact, of what our commanders had been prepared to accept.

And these units that were so battered and went through such hell are still, right at this moment, pushing on inland without rest, their spirits high, their egotism in victory almost reaching the smart-alecky stage.

Their tails are up. "We've done it again," they say. They figure that the rest of the army isn't needed at all. Which proves that, while their judgment in this regard is bad, they certainly have the spirit that wins battles and eventually wars.

THE HORRIBLE WASTE OF WAR

NORMANDY BEACHHEAD, JUNE 16, 1944—
I took a walk along the historic coast of Normandy in the country of France.

It was a lovely day for strolling along the seashore. Men were sleeping on the sand, some of them sleeping forever. Men were floating in the water, but they didn't know they were in the water, for they were dead.

The water was full of squishy little jellyfish about the size of your hand. Millions of them. In the center each of them had a green design exactly like a four-leaf clover. The good-luck emblem. Sure. Hell yes.

I walked for a mile and a half along the water's edge of our many-miled invasion beach. You wanted to walk slowly, for the detail on that beach was infinite.

The wreckage was vast and startling. The awful waste and destruction of war, even aside from the loss of human life, has always been one of its outstanding features to those who are in it. Anything and everything is expendable. And we did expend on our beachhead in Normandy during those first few hours.

. . .

For a mile out from the beach there were scores of tanks and trucks and boats that you could no longer see, for they were at the bottom of the water—swamped by overloading, or hit by shells, or sunk by mines. Most of their crews were lost.

You could see trucks tipped half over and swamped. You could see partly sunken barges, and the angled-up corners of jeeps, and small landing craft half submerged. And at low tide you could still see those vicious six-pronged iron snares that helped snag and wreck them.

On the beach itself, high and dry, were all kinds of wrecked vehicles. There were tanks that had only just made the beach before being knocked out. There were jeeps that had been burned to a dull gray. There were big derricks on caterpillar treads that didn't quite make it. There were half-tracks carrying office equipment that had been made into a shambles by a single shell hit, their interiors still holding their useless equipage of smashed typewriters, telephones, office files.

There were LCT's turned completely upside down, and lying on their backs, and how they got that way I don't know. There were boats stacked on top of each other, their sides caved in, their suspension doors knocked off.

In this shoreline museum of carnage there were abandoned rolls of barbed wire and smashed bulldozers and big stacks of thrown-away lifebelts and piles of shells still waiting to be moved.

In the water floated empty life rafts and soldiers' packs and ration boxes, and mysterious oranges.

On the beach lay snarled rolls of telephone wire and big rolls of steel matting and stacks of broken, rusting rifles.

On the beach lay, expended, sufficient men and mechanism for a small war. They were gone forever now. And yet we could afford it.

We could afford it because we were on, we had our toehold, and behind us there were such enormous replacements for this wreckage on the beach that you could hardly conceive of their sum total. Men and equipment were flowing from England in such a gigantic stream that it made the waste on the beachhead seem like nothing at all, really nothing at all.

A few hundred yards back on the beach is a high bluff. Up there we had a tent hospital, and a barbed-wire enclosure for prisoners of war. From up there you could see far up and down the beach, in a spectacular crow's-nest view, and far out to sea.

And standing out there on the water beyond all this wreckage was the greatest armada man has ever seen. You simply could not believe the gigantic collection of ships that lay out there waiting to unload.

Looking from the bluff, it lay thick and clear to the far horizon of the sea and beyond, and it spread out to the sides and was miles wide. Its utter enormity would move the hardest man.

As I stood up there I noticed a group of freshly taken German prisoners standing nearby. They had not yet been put in the prison cage. They were just standing there, a couple of doughboys leisurely guarding them with tommy guns.

The prisoners too were looking out to sea— the same bit of sea that for months and years had been so safely empty before their gaze. Now they stood staring almost as if in a trance.

They didn't say a word to each other. They didn't need to. The expression on their faces was something forever unforgettable. In it was the final horrified acceptance of their doom.

If only all Germans could have had the rich experience of standing on the bluff and looking out across the water and seeing what their compatriots saw.

A LONG THIN LINE OF PERSONAL ANGUISH

NORMANDY BEACHHEAD, JUNE 17, 1944— In the preceding column we told about the D-day wreckage among our machines of war that were expended in taking one of the Normandy beaches.

But there is another and more human litter. It

extends in a thin little line, just like a high-water mark, for miles along the beach. This is the strewn personal gear, gear that will never be needed again, of those who fought and died to give us our entrance into Europe.

Here in a jumbled row for mile on mile are soldiers' packs. Here are socks and shoe polish, sewing kits, diaries, Bibles and hand grenades. Here are the latest letters from home, with the address on each one neatly razored out—one of the security precautions enforced before the boys embarked.

Here are toothbrushes and razors, and snapshots of families back home staring up at you from the sand. Here are pocketbooks, metal mirrors, extra trousers, and bloody, abandoned shoes. Here are broken-handled shovels, and portable radios smashed almost beyond recognition, and mine detectors twisted and ruined.

Here are torn pistol belts and canvas water buckets, first-aid kits and jumbled heaps of lifebelts. I picked up a pocket Bible with a soldier's name in it, and put it in my jacket. I carried it half a mile or so and then put it back down on the beach. I don't know why I picked it up, or why I put it back down.

Soldiers carry strange things ashore with them. In every invasion you'll find at least one soldier hitting the beach at H-hour with a banjo slung over his shoulder. The most ironic piece of equipment marking our beach—this beach of first despair, then victory—is a tennis racket that some soldier had brought along. It lies lonesomely on the sand, clamped in its rack, not a string broken.

Two of the most dominant items in the beach refuse are cigarets and writing paper. Each soldier was issued a carton of cigarets just before he started. Today these cartons by the thousand, water-soaked and spilled out, mark the line of our first savage blow.

Writing paper and air-mail envelopes come second. The boys had intended to do a lot of writing in France. Letters that would have filled those blank, abandoned pages.

Always there are dogs in every invasion. There is a dog still on the beach today, still pitifully looking for his masters.

He stays at the water's edge, near a boat that lies twisted and half sunk at the water line. He barks appealingly to every soldier who approaches, trots eagerly along with him for a few feet, and then, sensing himself unwanted in all this haste, runs back to wait in vain for his own people at his own empty boat.

Over and around this long thin line of personal anguish, fresh men today are rushing vast supplies to keep our armies pushing on into France. Other squads of men pick amidst the wreckage to salvage ammunition and equipment that are still usable.

Men worked and slept on the beach for days before the last D-day victim was taken away for burial.

I stepped over the form of one youngster whom I thought dead. But when I looked down I saw he was only sleeping. He was very young, and very tired. He lay on one elbow, his hand suspended in the air about six inches from the ground. And in the palm of his hand he held a large, smooth rock.

I stood and looked at him a long time. He seemed in his sleep to hold that rock lovingly, as though it were his last link with a vanishing world. I have no idea at all why he went to sleep with the rock in his hand, or what kept him from dropping it once he was asleep. It was just one of those little things without explanation that a person remembers for a long time.

The strong, swirling tides of the Normandy coastline shift the contours of the sandy beach as they move in and out. They carry soldiers' bodies out to sea, and later they return them. They cover the corpses of heroes with sand, and then in their whims they uncover them.

As I plowed out over the wet sand of the beach on that first day ashore, I walked around what seemed to be a couple of pieces of driftwood sticking out of the sand. But they weren't driftwood.

They were a soldier's two feet. He was completely covered by the shifting sands except for his feet. The toes of his GI shoes pointed toward the land he had come so far to see, and which he saw so briefly.

MEMORIES OF VIETNAM

by C. W. Bowman, Jr.

C. W. Bowman, Jr., served two tours of duty in Vietnam. His first essay records his memory of one short, intense fight. Known for being one of few true "tunnel rats" who risked exploring Vietcong tunnels during the war, he has appeared on a History Channel special on the tunnels and has continued to write and speak about his experiences during the war and the challenges he faced after he returned home. His second piece deals with his experiences in the tunnels.

THE BATTLE OF THE HORSESHOE

Hopefully my memory will serve me well in writing this account; after all it's been over thirty-two years since it happened. For Company B, 4/9th Manchus, the battle started the day before on August 29, 1967. We had been on an operation in the Iron Triangle for several days east of the river where it made a horseshoe turn and then flowed down to Saigon. Our unit was held up in an old rubber-tree plantation waiting for the order to move out, when we noticed several jets making bombing runs along the river. It was like sitting in a movie theater. We would watch the jets as they swooped in to deliver their ordinance, watch them fly off, then look for the explosion and cloud of smoke. We were told they had spotted a large VC

[Vietcong] force in that area and were trying to drop everything they had on them. Being infantry, we all thought this was much better than dropping us on top of them, though we were told later we would probably be going there tomorrow. It got a little scary sitting there because shrapnel from some of the larger bombs started to hit in our perimeter. You could hear the hot metal as it came buzzing in. It was hitting in the trees or it would hit in the soft ground where it left a smoking crater. Everyone moved behind the trees so as not to be a target for the flying metal. After several hours, word came that we would be extracted from our location, taken to Chu Chi for a stand-down, spend the night, and CA [combat assault] in the morning to where they were bombing along the river.

At about 1600 we saddled up and moved out of the tree line to a dirt road and waited for our extraction to Chu Chi. After about thirty minutes, we started receiving sniper fire from the west side of the road. As the choppers came in to extract us, the firing increased in tempo, hitting one of the choppers, causing it to auto-rotate about 200 meters down the road. Our squad was ordered to move out to secure the chopper, as we ran down the road with about 80 pounds of our gear on, all hell broke loose. There was automatic fire coming from where the chopper crashed, and the more we ran toward the downed chopper, the more intense it got. My heart was pounding so hard, I thought it was going to burst through my chest. I don't know if it was from trying to run with all my gear on or just fear. All I could think of was that I was running to my death. We finally got the chopper and secured it. None of the crew was killed or wounded, just had the hell scared out of them like the rest of us.

A Chinook was sent in to retrieve the downed chopper. We didn't receive any incoming fire, as they were rigging it up for extraction. I guess that's because they had gun ships making runs up and down both sides of the road. We got the downed crew aboard the Chinook, they lifted off, and we moved back to our original location along the road. Finding out that we were on the last lift out, we waited for the choppers to come back for us. Again we started to receive fire from the west side of the road; most of us just kept our heads down because the incoming fire wasn't that heavy or accurate. When the choppers approached the landing zone, the incoming fire intensified and we returned fire in earnest, all the time praying for the choppers to get us extracted out. As the choppers lifted off, the door gunner on my side opened up with his M-60 and pointed toward a spot about thirty meters out from my old position. There lay three dead VC he'd just shot. Nothing like a hot extraction to get your adrenaline flowing.

Returning to Chu Chi, we were told to get our

gear cleaned up, get new ammo, and be ready to go to the Horseshoe in the morning. As we were getting ready, word was passed they were going to fire about 6,000 rounds of artillery into the area before we CAed, it would be a walk in the park returning to Chu Chi by noon. After hearing this, most of us didn't collect any C-rations or plan to take any extra gear since we would be back by noon. After getting our gear ready, we went to the EM [enlisted men's] club to drink a few beers, and if I remember right, I won ten dollars on the dime slot machine. Later, several of us walked over to Delta Company area to see the new guys. The whole company was just brought into the country, and most of the guys were green except for the old timers taken out of some other companies and mixed in with them. We thought we would talk to them for a while because they were to make the CA with us in the morning. We stood around smoking and joking and told the guys it would be a walk in the park for them. Gary Heeter, Paul Frisbee, and myself decided to go back to our hooch to get some sleep. We had to be on the chopper pad at 0700.

Waking up around 0600, we went to the mess hall for chow: the usual bacon, eggs, and whatever, with a lot of coffee. Everyone was feeling good because this was going to be an easy morning to make a CA and be back by noon. After eating, we went to our hooch to get our gear and move out to the chopper pad. We were all laughing and talking crap on the way to the pad. What the hell, they bombed the place the day before and fired 6,000 rounds of artillery on it before we went in. Hey, walk in the park! Alpha Company was to go in on the first lift, followed by Bravo, Delta, and then Charlie Company last. We waited on the pad for the choppers to come back and get us after they lifted in Alpha Company. We didn't have to wait long, and we didn't know it at the time, but two choppers didn't make it back for our lift. We loaded up as usual. I always sat on the end of the bench next to the door gunner. As we lifted off, I remember looking into the sky and saying to myself, "Well, Lord, I'm in your hands now. Here's another chapter in my life." As we approached the LZ [landing zone], I tapped the door gunner on the shoulder, yelling over the rotor noise, asking if it was a hot LZ. The door gunner started nodding his head up and down and pointed toward the LZ, where I saw a chopper on the ground burning. About the same time, rounds started to hit our chopper and pieces of metal started falling off. We were still a good ways away from the LZ when a round came into the chopper between me and the door gunner and hit the guy next to me in the neck. About the same time I saw a piece of the door frame disappear, and then it got really bad. It sounded like someone was beating the hell out of the chopper with a big hammer. All the time I was wishing we could get on the ground before we were knocked out of the sky. As the chopper flared, it started to vibrate like hell, and we jumped out into mud up to our waist, leaving the wounded man on board.

The mud was like quicksand because of all the artillery and bombs dropped into the area the previous day and that morning. I was trying to free myself from the mud when I looked back and saw a tail rotor coming straight for me at ground level. Tears sprang to my eyes because I knew the rotor was going to hit me. I was going to die. God must have been with me because the rotor missed me by about five feet. I really don't know how to explain what happened unless the pilot tried to lift the nose of the chopper and turn because of the downed chopper in the LZ. I can't tell you how relieved I was when the chopper flew off. Our next problem was that several of us were up to our hips in mud with rounds hitting all around us. We had to lie down in the mud and kind of swim through it to get to a berm behind us about ten to fifteen meters. Making it to the berm, we crawled over it into a depression with AK [-47] rounds, and B-40 rockets hitting right behind us. Things really got crazy by then, gunships were hitting the wood line with mini-guns and rockets, and we were firing everything we had, trying to suppress the incoming fire for the next chopper lift due to arrive any time.

The choppers flew in to the rear of us, a little

outside of the horseshoe to drop off Delta Company. The whole time you could hear the intensity of the firing increase until it sounded like a giant buzz saw gone crazy. We kept up the fire until Delta Company was on the ground and the choppers lifted off. One of the choppers flew out between us and the wood line about fifteen feet above the ground. As I watched, the door gunner got shot and fell forward, hanging by his monkey strap. I always wondered if the VC shot him or if it was one of us during the heat of battle. After the flight left, they had us expand our perimeter to link up with the Alpha and Delta Companies. Charlie Company never got in the fight. So many of the choppers were shot up they didn't have enough birds left to bring them in. As we moved through the high grass, you could actually hear the incoming rounds cutting grass, the subsonic crack as they passed by your head. The man next to me was shot in the hand; we helped get him to our new position and bandaged him up. I remember there were so many snipers that you had to crawl wherever you went. If you stood up, you died on the spot.

Alpha Company had already assaulted the wood line into the bend of the horseshoe and retreated back to the paddies, with several dead and wounded under heavy fire. Next, Delta Company assaulted the lower right side of the horseshoe and was repelled with heavy fire from the VC, falling back into the paddies. Several of the dead and wounded were not recovered until the next day. Bravo Company was pinned down by intensive fire and couldn't go anywhere and laid in the paddies behind what protection they could find.

The CO [commanding officer] called artillery and had a ring of steel placed around us. You could hear the rounds leave the tube at Chu Chi and whistle over your head on the way to the wood line. They started firing 105s, then 155s, next 175s, and finally, eight-inchers. It sounded like the whole world was blowing up around us. The ground would roll and shake as the concussion from the explosions would roll over us. In between the artillery, air strikes and gunships were called in to support us to suppress incoming fire. I remember the F-4s coming in so low you could see the pilot as they flew by. They would come in from the east and release their bombs; it scared the Hell out of us because it looked like we were going to get hit. They were dropping snake-eye bombs, 750 pounds. When released, the fins would pop open. They would wobble over our heads, hitting the wood line in front of us. We were bouncing up and down from the shock waves as shrapnel flew all over the place. When the F-4s made a run and opened fire with their 20-millimeter cannon, the wood line looked like it was melting. The empty casings would fall among us, and if one hit you, it hurt like hell. Luckily no one was killed.

Later that morning we received word they

were going to try to get some of the wounded out and to be ready to put out suppressive fire. Looking behind us in the distance, I saw one of the craziest or bravest things I ever saw during the war. A Canberra jet with a gunship on his right side was heading straight for our perimeter with a medevac chopper underneath them. When they got in close, both the Canberra and the gunship opened up with their guns, one firing 7.65-millimeter, the other firing 20-millimeter, into the wood line in front of us. At the same time, the medevac swooped in underneath both ships trying to get the wounded out. I believe that was the only dust-off to get in that day. He got shot up real bad, but made it out again. I know choppers did fly in to bring us ammo and water. I don't know for sure; I think they had to kick our supplies out as they flew over because of intense fire. Lying in the mud all morning while the sun burned us up, we still couldn't move around because of all the snipers.

Later a squad leader crawled over to me and asked me to move to the berm behind us, because I carried an M-79 grenade launcher. They had spotted some bunkers and wanted me to put some rounds into them. I crawled over to the location, thinking that's the last time I ever wanted to carry an M-79. I finally got there and they asked "if I could put some smoke rounds on top of the bunkers so they could call in air strikes on them." I had several smoke rounds and a few night flares;

I didn't want to fire any of my HE [high-explosive] rounds because I only had a few of them left. Also, it would have been a waste of time because the bunkers were so thick.

I fired a couple of smoke rounds and Charlie must have gotten wise to what I was doing because a round from a sniper hit a tree next to my head. I fell to the ground and pretended I was hit and crawled to a new location to fire my next round. I finally ran out of smoke rounds and tried to use my night flares. Now that was funny. When I fired a flare, the little chute would open and it would float to the ground in front of the bunker. We didn't knock out any bunkers with this trick, and I finally ran out of smoke and illumination rounds. So I saved what HE rounds I had in case we had to assault the wood line again.

Then we just laid there most of the day, trading shots back and forth, burning up from the heat. I had more rounds for my M-79 brought up from Delta Company's area. We had a guy that could speak some Vietnamese and every time it got quiet he would holler over to the Vietnamese that Ho Chi Minh was an MF, or several other choice words. After doing this several times, it got quiet and before he could holler again, a VC from the wood line yelled out that President Johnson was a son of a bitch. We all broke up laughing.

At about 1600 hours, the squad leaders came around and told us to get ready to assault the wood line one more time. When we got the order to move out, we fired everything we had at the wood line, and began our assault. I got within thirty meters of the wood line when I saw a trail of bullets to my right walk past me and head to the wood line. I turned and saw a U.S. gunship headed straight for our group, firing his mini-guns. It scared the hell out of everyone; we all started throwing smoke grenades, hoping they would break off their attack. Finally the chopper broke off his attack, and everyone began running out of the wood line back to our old positions. I picked myself up and ran with them. I think only one man was wounded from the chopper incident. After we got back to our old positions, we were told we were going to spend the night in place and make an assault in the morning while they walked artillery to the front of us.

It was a long night in the paddies. The tide rose, flooding the area. We were all soaking wet and covered with leeches. A lot of us felt like we were freezing to death because of the wetness and drop in temperature. We didn't bring any poncho liners, extra equipment, or C rations because we thought we would be out of the field by noon. It was pretty damn miserable. We lay there all night cold, hungry, and watching for Charlie. They fired illumination over us all night, and H&I [harassment and interdiction] off and on. We just laid there in the water and mud, praying for the sun to come up. We didn't receive any incoming that night, maybe because just before dark several jets came in and dropped anti-personnel bomblets around our perimeter. It was a hell of a fireworks display all day long.

Just before daylight, our squad leader told us to get ready to assault the wood line; artillery was coming in about fifteen minutes. At the crack of dawn, you could hear the big guns firing back at Chu Chi, the rounds fluttering over your head as they passed over striking the wood line. Trees were exploding from hits; mud and logs were flying up into the sky. The first thing I thought of was the old TV show *Combat!* I used to watch when I was younger. Then something really strange happened. As I was standing there waiting for the word to move out, it was like I stepped outside of my body, standing to the side, looking at myself. It lasted only for a few seconds, but I walked around myself, then stepped back into my body in time to hear the squad leader say move out.

It was a nightmare. The troops trying to move through the mud, artillery blowing up everything in front of us, us firing everything we had into the wood line, the whole area covered with a haze of smoke. I finally noticed we were not receiving any return fire, which made everyone happy to say the least. The VC had moved out during the night. The bunkers were empty and I think we only found four dead VC. I know my squad didn't find any bodies, and that was very discouraging because of all the fighting the previous day. We continued sweeping the area, not finding anything. We decided to set up along a tidal creek that flowed into the main river. As we were digging in, two guys on the other side of the perimeter dug up two automatic weapons wrapped in plastic, so we knew the enemy wasn't far away. As we got ready to spend the night, I sprayed myself with a can of mosquito repellant. Not only would it keep the bugs and leeches off; it would also irritate my skin and keep me warm all night. We didn't make contact that night and in the morning they brought in Chinooks to lift us out back to Chu Chi.

They told us the 1/27 Wolfhounds were sent in as a reaction force to support us, and that Charlie Company never did get into the fight. Of the three companies that were in the fight, I think there were fourteen KIAs [killed in action] and forty-five WIAs [wounded in action]. I don't know the name or unit number of the VC outfit we fought against, nor the names of those who were killed and wounded. All I do know: it was no walk in the park.

"Sometime this year you will go crazy!
Don't piss anyone off—we all carry guns!
Don't worry about the bullet with your
name on it. It's the one that says anybody,
anybody, that will kill you!
Don't make friends!
If you live through the year, you will not
go home the same person!"

These were the first words out of our senior field leader's mouth when we reported to our unit in Vietnam.

Our unit was Company B, Fourth Battallion, Ninth Infantry, 25th Infantry Division, Second Platoon. Our call sign was Manchu; our company was Bravo. Of course we didn't pay any attention to the field leader's words, and I didn't realize how right he was until later in the war. I reported to the unit on January 10, 1967. This was my first tour; one tour was twelve months. I was in the early part of the war, one of the first replacements in our unit. I tried to hang around the old-timers to learn everything I could about staying alive. The problem was the old-timers didn't want anything to do with you because you were an FNG (fucking new guy) and they didn't trust you with their lives. The saying in Vietnam was that you would most likely die in the first ninety days or the last ninety days of your tour—the first ninety days because you didn't know anything, the last ninety because you were overcautious; there was a lot of truth in that saying.

By January 30th, I had been wounded along with several others, and some didn't make it at all. I was only twenty days into my tour wondering how in the hell I was going to make it the rest of the way.

Now, if you want to stay alive, you start to make the change. Forget about your family, girlfriend, or whatever at home—they are a distraction. Thinking about them will get you killed. Get rid of any of your feelings, become hard about killing someone, and prepare to die yourself. You can't shoot someone you like. You have to pay attention to what is going on. There was a point in Vietnam where I actually felt I had been born there and had lived there all of my life. I had to take out photos of my brothers, my parents, to remember what they looked like. I needed to get rid of anything that would distract me.

If you're real lucky you will develop a good sixth sense about things going on around you. The last problem you have is the friends you made when you first arrived here. We lived and died for each other, and when one of them died, part of you died with them, and made you that much harder. You never learned the new guys' names because if they died, you didn't know them and it didn't hurt.

Strange things start happening to you when

you're in combat a lot. I mention a sixth sense. Not everyone developed a sixth sense, but some of us did. This not only saved me several times but my squad and platoon also. I can't explain it, but it really made me feel special. I could feel things around me. Such as I could look and spot booby traps, entrances to tunnels, sense where there was an ambush waiting for us. With this ability I ended up walking point for my unit most of the time. Point man is the guy who walks out in front of the unit usually 50 to 100 meters to spot booby traps or ambushes. This is where I guess it started with the adrenaline rushes. It really felt great if something happened and you lived through it. Your heart pounding, the hair standing up on your neck, the feeling of really being alive. I guess it wasn't enough for me because I started running tunnels, along with a guy named Gary Heeter.

The Vietnamese started building tunnels when they were fighting against the French, in the 1950s. By the time I got there, the tunnels had many levels; some ran as many as sixty miles long—they had rooms, hospitals, trapdoors, and many tricks for trapping and killing any enemies who came into them. They would nail vipers to a board hanging over a tunnel entrance, so anyone who did not know and crawled in would be bitten and killed. They would wait just above a door between levels, then ram a rod through the neck of anyone who climbed through—so he could neither go up nor down, and his buddies below would be blocked by his body, and hear him scream.

The first tunnel I went into was really a large bunker that had an exit you could see from the entrance. They handed me a flashlight with a red lens and told me to check out the bunker. I guess by this time I didn't have any brains because this stuff was strictly voluntary and I didn't have to do this, but I did. The inside of the bunker was the blackest black I ever encountered; the red lens on the light couldn't penetrate the blackness. All I could see was the little bit of light coming in on the other side of the bunker; all I could hear was my heart pounding in my ears. At first I couldn't move—it was like my feet and legs weighed a thousand pounds. I kept telling myself that if I could make it to the light I would live. My feet began to move forward. I didn't look left or right but only at the light, thinking I had to make it to the light. Finally with my heart pounding so hard I thought it would burst, I made it to the exit into daylight. What a feeling—I was alive, and it got better as I started to run more tunnels.

From then on whenever our unit found a tunnel, they called Gary and me to run it. This was not for everyone. Some other guys tried to go in with me and would freeze as we entered the tunnel. It was nothing to be ashamed of: this was strictly voluntary, and Gary and I were the only ones in our unit doing it. One important thing to remember is if you got into trouble in a tunnel, no one was going to come to your rescue. As time went by, Gary and I went into more and more tunnels. Gary always told me he went with me because he felt safe that I was there. I would strip to the waist— just pants and boots, a flashlight, and a .45-caliber pistol. I usually went in first, with Gary backing me up. As time went by, the pounding in my heart slowed down to where I could hear; I could feel every grain of sand and every trickle of sweat on my body. I always held my flashlight in my left hand extended out and to the left of me, so if someone shot at the light, they wouldn't hit me. The problem was most tunnels didn't have that much room to do this. After a while Paul Frisbee told me the guys in our platoon were betting that I wouldn't live through my tour. Gary and I had a mystique about us; we were now the crazies, and no one would mess with us.

As time went by, things got worse. Your friends were gone—dead or wounded so bad they were sent home—and here you sat and wondered why not me. Gary stepped on a Bouncing Betty and was ripped apart; he lived but was severely injured. My other close friend, Paul, was gone, transferred to another unit. I was alone, and didn't care anymore. Every day people were dying and being blown apart by booby traps and still I lived. Why? One sergeant was hit in the head with a rocket-propelled grenade; it took his head off. When he fell, he fell on his knees. The blast literally blew his face off. I wanted to say good-bye. But I couldn't talk to him—I didn't know whether to hug the body or speak to the face. So I turned around and walked away. That is what war is.

I began running tunnels by myself. It got crazy—I don't think I wanted to die, but I didn't care about living either. I was the old man of the unit; I was twenty years old and didn't care anymore about myself. But I did care about the young guys—they had wives, girlfriends, families to go home to. I really didn't, so I started to volunteer for point man, ambush patrol, to run tunnels, anything to keep these guys alive another day. You could say I did go crazy, or I was just stupid or foolish—you make the call.

I would volunteer to go on night ambush for weeks at a time, walk point, no problem. I have even gone into tunnels with a stick in one hand and flashlight in the other with my pistol in my back pocket (who would be fastest on the draw if I met the enemy?). Adrenaline rush, crazy, death wish— it's your call, because I really didn't give a damn.

Some tunnels were so tight that you had to crawl through them; in others you could stand. One day I was walking through a tunnel, turned a corner, and walked into a room. It was a hospital, with beds made of bamboo, men lying on them, and their weapons stacked up against the wall. I stopped. They looked at me. I looked at them. I started shooting, backing out. I was terrified. I had only seven rounds in the pistol, then it locked back. I was so scared getting out that, halfway out, the fear turned to anger. I didn't want my buddies to know how scared I had been. I got thirty pounds of plastic explosive, set a charge, dropped it three levels down to the hospital, then shut the door. Standing back on the ground, I felt a little tremble, a small muffled boom. I could not go back; all of the oxygen had been sucked out of the tunnel by the explosion.

You don't fight for God, for country; you do it for your buddies, and they are doing it for you, trying to keep each other alive. You are scared to death; you are thinking, "I'm going to die, going to die, going to die." I can't say it's like butterflies before a football game; it's worse. But once you are in action, your reaction takes over. You don't have time to think about it. You are trying to keep your buddies alive; they are trying to keep you alive. A closeness develops that's beyond brothers, a friendship that can only be found in battle.

That is what gives you the ability when they say, "Fix bayonets; get on line," and you are in an open field, and there's woods over there, and you are walking toward that wood line, knowing that there could be 1,000 troops waiting, waiting for you to get 10 or 15 meters away before opening fire, to follow the order. Or if you are going through the jungle and you walk into an ambush, rather than lie down, you have to assault the ambush, break the ambush. The enemy is literally shooting the place to pieces, but you charge to break them. If you don't, everybody dies. You know some will die, some will be wounded, but the majority will live if you charge; otherwise everybody dies.

I learned a lot from Vietnam: I realized that you have to work together; you have to read other people's minds. I became a factual person.

You have to go insane to fight in war. The key is to come out of it after it is over. It took me years to do that. When I came back, I would drive at a hundred miles an hour at night with the headlights off, just to get the same rush I had going into the tunnels. In 1998, I went back to Vietnam and met some of the Vietnamese I had known. I went to dinner with the woman who used to sell us sodas. When I left her home, I could not speak for almost an hour. I realized they were human. I had developed the mentality to kill them; now I saw them as suffering human beings like I was, people who had lost families, children.

The worst part of Vietnam for me was coming home. Everyone was afraid of me, even my family. My relatives were so scared of me, that if they had to wake me up, they poked me with a broom handle so they wouldn't have to be near me. I did not feel at home again, until, just thirty days after getting back, I returned to Vietnam to fight again. I knew that was crazy, but it was how I felt.

If I were talking to a teenager today thinking of going to fight I'd say, Are you cut out for it? Some people are; some are not. War is the worst thing ever. You'll have to see and do things no man should ever have to face. There has to be a cause that you believe in, and an ending for the war. But if your country really is in danger, you have to ask yourself, "What is your country worth to you?" I felt my country needed me, that it was my time.

If I met a soldier who was just back from Iraq or some other combat today, I'd buy him a drink, say welcome home. And then I'd say, "How are you doing?" I don't mean, "Are you wounded physically?" but, "How are you doing mentally? If you need some help, don't let it linger, 'cause one day you are going to wake up and start crying and not know why. You will have a pistol in one hand and a bottle of pills in the other, and you will be laughing and crying, not knowing should you blow your brains out or overdose. 'What is wrong with me?' you'll ask. And it will be everything you've been through that you've suppressed, that you made yourself forget."

LETTERS FROM VIETNAM

by Mickey Andrews

Mickey Andrews was drafted into the U.S. Army on June 24, 1968. He arrived in South Vietnam on November 16, 1968, as a replacement and was assigned to Company A, 2/22nd Mechanized Infantry Battalion, 25th Infantry Division, operating in the Third Brigade area of operations around Dau Tieng base camp, near the Michelin and Ben Cui rubber plantations in Tay Ninh province. He was wounded on January 8, 1969, in an ambush while he was on reconnaissance patrol in a jungle area known as the Boi Loi Woods. He was medevaced out of Vietnam and back to Fort Campbell in Kentucky. He was hospitalized from January 8, 1969, to April 7, 1969, due to multiple shrapnel wounds to his neck and both legs resulting from two rocket-propelled grenade explosions during the ambush. He later attended Auburn University, in Alabama, from which he graduated with a B.S. degree in pharmacy in December 1973. Mickey is married to wife Dorothy, has two daughters, Daina and Barrie, and one granddaughter, Taylor. He has been employed by the Department of Veterans Affairs at Central Alabama Veterans Health Care System since January 1975.

December 22, 1968

Dear Mom and Doc,

How is everything in the world nowadays? Are you still having occasional snow? I received your package. I ate the pineapple already. I haven't received that watch battery, so maybe I threw it away and didn't know it. Did you send it with anything else? I'll be sending you about three roles of film soon. I hope they turn out. A couple are good action shots taken by our driver.

Seems like I'm losing things right and left. I've now lost both my pair of regular glasses, and my gas mask was stolen. I've got another mask now. Today, Gary Ray and I checked some area out in front of our OP [observation post]. I put a mask on and went around pouring CS gas [tear gas] in the VC [Vietcong] fighting holes. Gary and Roy set fire to the grass and trees. We all enjoy setting fires.

Doc, Steve (our medic) is in bad need of Band-Aids. You know how the army supply system is. Here we have to scrounge around for everything. So if you got any Band-Aids or anything else helpful, please send some. Doc said he would appreciate it very much, because he is dedicated to helping us when we need him. We couldn't get along without him.

I'm getting all sorts of Christmas cards. People from La Follette are sending me some even. I've had two from young girls. Roma Shelby sent me one, also. I'm sorry I didn't have a chance to eat that Santa Claus cookie. The damn ants beat me to it. Thanks for the mosquito repellant—I definitely needed it. Now I can sleep in peace.

Last nite we had a band from the Philippines entertain us. It was a Rock n Roll group, and they were really good. We all had a great time. Every time a 155 mm gun would go off, those Filipinos almost jumped off the stage. We would be laughing at them, because we're so used to it. The other night, Mike and I were sitting in a club drinking Cokes. Everything was real quiet, and we were talking about home. All of a sudden a big 155 mm howitzer went off about 30 yards away. We almost went under the table. I thought a mortar had hit us for sure.

What were you all doing the 17th and 18th of December? I earned my CIB [Combat Infantryman Badge]. I was on the .50 cal. [.50-caliber machine gun] and poured about 1100 rounds at the gooks. My squad leader said I did a real fine job. I really like that gun. Gary's platoon killed four gooks on the 19th. But an RPG [rocket-propelled grenade] hit Gary's track [armored personnel vehicle]. Nobody was seriously injured. Gary caught a small piece of shrapnel under the eye—not bad, though. I've been kidding him about getting a Purple Heart.

I'm getting to know my way around more now. Before I had no confidence that I could do anything over here, but now I set out trip flares, claymore mines, talk over the radio, fire the .50 cal. machine gun and the M-60. I'm learning the ways of war, because someday whether I want it or not, I'll be a squad leader. I want to know what to do.

I'm sharing most of my Christmas with the baby-*sans* (kids). We go through a village and throw the kids candy as we pass by. Some of them are really cute. These kids are something else. They line the roads every morning hollering "chop chop." I gave one little girl a half a can of peanuts. She thought it was really a meaningful gift. I promised two little sisters that the next time I come through the village I would give them a can of candy. They watched me when we drove off, and they are probably still standing there waiting for me. They never forget a person. They won't let me take their picture. We all have a time playing around with these kids, especially Doc. He's their favorite.

Wow! The jets are giving the gooks hell. Pour it to them! It's like watching a show.

I'll close for now. I'm in good spirits and doing fine. Have a Merry Christmas, and take care of yourselves. Thanks for all the packages and their contents.

Be writing again soon.

Love,

Mick

January 1, 1969

Mom and Doc,

How was Christmas at the various places? Happy New Year! We celebrated by shooting off star clusters and flares. We are now in another logger [camp] about 3 miles outside of Dau Tieng. We are supposed to be here for 30 days.

I saw the Bob Hope Show at Chu Chi! Mike and I were sent to pick up an APC [armored personnel carrier] and it took a while, so we got to see Bob Hope. I was really lucky to be able to see the show. Mike drove the track back in a convoy with me as the .50 gunner. We went through several small villages of Interstate 554 North into Dau Tieng. We passed through Trang Bang and another famous VC village. The scenery was pretty and it felt like I was on a Sunday drive. Some of the road was paved, but most of the way we endured the dust and bumps. I wish I had taken some pictures of the countryside.

I'm in the same old routine—building bunkers, laying wire, riffing [patrolling] and so forth. We are driving through jungles and places you can't believe a vehicle could go through. It's like riding a roller coaster sometimes.

We have the day off today, so I'm having the opportunity to write this letter. I really received a lot of mail from people. Jim Hampton, Jane Stubblefield, the Hamptons, the Edwards, my Sunday school class, Uncle Doyle, MaMa, Douglas Jerry, Charlie Glover, the Coleys (Randall), and from people I never knew.

Charlie was in that convoy ambush my platoon reacted to the 17th of December. I heard from him the other day and we compared notes. He comes into Dau Tieng most every day escorting convoys.

Ray is going out of the field in a few days. Mike will be our squad leader and Gary will be our driver. In another month Gary will take Mike's place as squad leader and I'll be the driver probably. Can you imagine me driving a 13-ton army vehicle? I can't.

Well, I'd best be taking myself a bath. It's been 9 days since I've had one. My clothes are a mess. I'm enclosing a picture of myself holding an M-60 machine gun. My track is in the background. I'll send some more along when I can. For now I'll close. I'll write soon as I can.

Love,
Mick

January 9, 1969
Dear Mom + Doc,
I don't know whether or not you have been told by the army or not, but I'm in the hospital for a while. I don't feel much like talking about it, but I wanted you all to know I'm going to be OK. A Lieutenant Colonel came by my bed and gave me my Purple Heart. Receiving it just isn't worth the sacrifice. I'm awful lucky. Ray Bain, Mike Groves, Mike Metten, Gary Ledbetter, Andy Gabert, Barella, and myself were all wounded. When I'm feeling better, I'll tell you the story.

I'm now at Chu Chi, but I don't know if I'll stay here long. I may be sent to Japan—I sure hope so. At least I'm out of the war for a month or two. I wish I could go home, but they won't let me go that far.

Don't write me until I can find out about how my mail works. Maybe they will forward my mail from my unit.

I'm in a nice bed in an air-conditioned building. There is 3 good meals a day, a couple of good-looking women lieutenants (nurses), cold sodas, and a TV. I'm in a pretty good place. Ray is in another ward and will be sent to Japan, then the world. He only had 64 days to go when he got hit.

I lost my bracelet, knife, camera, film, and everything else I had on the track. It caught fire and blew up. Only one burned-out side was left. Van Pelt and Andy dropped in to say hello. They filled me in on everything. It happened so fast.

I'll be sending my Purple Heart home. I hope that's the only one I get. It's supposed to make you feel proud. Right now I don't care to even look at it. Take good care of it for me. I'm borrowing some of the medic's stationery, so I better not use too much. I'll let you know how everything is coming along. The doctor said I'm not hurt bad, so don't worry. I should be walking around in a week or so. I'll close for now. Hope everything if is fine with you. Take care.

Love,
Mickey

January 19, 1969
Dear Mom + Doc,
It's Sunday afternoon here, and the sun is shin-ing. I wished I could get up and roam about,

but I'm not allowed to walk for at least a week. Saturday morning the doc sewed up my leg. He gave me a spinal for the operation, so therefore I had to lie flat on my back for 24 hours after surgery. I have stainless steel wire holding my sewed-up places together. Believe me, it's mucho uncomfortable. I have a tube in one of my big holes to allow for drainage. I looked at my wounds before they closed them and after—rather ugly! But I'm too grateful to be alive to let it bother me. The stitches in my neck were taken out today, also. The scar is thin.

I'm coming home, people. How's does that sound? Thank God, I'm coming home. The doctor told me a few days ago, but I thought it best not to tell you just in case he changed his mind. But I think it's safe to say I'll be home before too long.

After I spend three weeks in Japan, I'll be flown to a hospital close to home (Fort Campbell), then a few days later I'll be given convalescent leave. God sure has been good to me. I'll miss Tet on February 19th, plus maybe I won't go back if Nixon can swing things right. It will be great to be able to walk in a civilized world again. I won't crouch every time I hear an explosion. I won't have to hit the ground when I hear a rifle shot. No mosquitoes, no heat, no jungle, no ants, no sweat. I can take a good warm shower for a change.

I'm in a new ward now. The guy on my left is a sergeant who got hit in the arm by an AK-47. The guy on my right is a marine, and my good buddy. We kid each other all the time. He wasn't wounded, but had to have an operation on some sort of external growth. We spend all day cutting each other's branch of service. He doesn't have much ground to boast, because he was drafted into the marines. He just brought me a couple of 7-Ups from the snack bar.

Suppose I'll cease. But I had to tell you I was coming home. I'm in a big hurry to see the U.S. again. I hope I never leave it again.

Chow!

Love,

Mickey

January 20, 1969

Dear Mom and Dad,

HAPPY BIRTHDAY TO ME! Twenty-two years young today. What a crazy place to spend one's birthday—in a hospital. The Captain (Doc) came by to look at my leg this morning. There was some infection in it, so he took the stitches out and left the wound open again. It was the biggest hole I had. The rest are all right. He said he'll sew it up again in three weeks. In the meantime I'm not allowed to run in any races. (HA!)

A finance clerk dropped by to give me $40 casualty pay. I now have money to pay for a haircut. I haven't had a haircut in nearly six weeks, so you can imagine what it looks like.

Did you receive my Purple Heart yet? Linda (a Red Cross girl) said she would send it to you for me. How was it wrapped and was there a card or letter attached with it? If so what did it say? Be sure to take good care of it—I went through a lot to get it. (HA!)

A person ought to be in an army hospital full of wounded GIs. If everybody could see the pain, fear, and hurt these guys have endured, maybe war would cease. Every night I can hear guys having nightmares or tossing and groaning with pain. Some of these men have no arms, or legs, or eyes, or half of their stomach is gone, or they are paralyzed. I'm so lucky to be wounded where I was. One guy has a hole through his leg big enough to drop a golf ball through. Plus he has stitches all the way up one side of his leg and down the other side. He stepped on a punji stick [a type of booby trap].

My neck is looking pretty good. I still have to feel every now and then to make sure I have my left ear. The side of my neck and head are still numb. I can turn my head, but it feels funny. By the time you get this letter it will make two weeks that I've been lying on my back or on my right side. Personally I'm ready to get up and romp around.

Well, the nurses are improving. The captain on night shift is a 23-year-old Panamanian. She also has a little Chinese blood in her. She gave me a back massage last night.

I'm running out of stationery, which a Red Cross woman gave me so it may be a while before I write again. I take that back—a Red Cross woman just came by taking orders for the PX [post exchange; a store on base], so she'll get me some stationery. It's been four days since I shaved—mainly because of no shaving cream, so I told her to purchase some for me. Ron (my marine buddy) just gave me a 7-Up to help celebrate my birthday. Tonight we are going to have a pizza party.

It's nearing chow time. I'll write again in a couple of days. I'll buy a Japanese camera and take some pictures when I'm able.

Chow!

Love,

Mickey Ray

WOMEN AT WAR

WHAT IT IS LIKE TO BE A FEMALE SOLDIER IN IRAQ

by Helen Benedict

Helen Benedict is a professor of journalism at Columbia University and the author of three novels for adults, as well as a young adult novel, The Opposite of Love. *This selection is adapted from her forthcoming book* The Lonely Soldier: Women at War in Iraq.

Mickiela Montoya is barely twenty-one years old and always on the verge of a giggle. She moves like a dancer, and her red hair falls in gentle waves around her wide-eyed, freckled face. It is hard to imagine her fighting in a war.

But that is exactly what she did in Iraq in 2005, as a specialist in the Army National Guard. She carried her M-16 rifle at all times, loaded and cleaned of the dusty Iraq sand. She guarded a checkpoint every night for months while being constantly shot at. She endured mortar attacks, from which there is no hiding. And, like more than 160,500 other women who have served in Iraq (one in every ten U.S. soldiers there is female), she witnessed death and mutilation all around her.

The Iraq War is producing a kind of female soldier America has rarely seen before. Like

Mickiela, she is frequently under hostile fire, and she is coming home with missing limbs, grave wounds, post-traumatic stress disorder—or in a body bag. As of January 2008, ninety-three American women soldiers have died in Iraq, over 544 have been wounded, and more than one in six is so traumatized that she cannot adjust to civilian life. More female soldiers have fought, died, and been wounded in Iraq than in Korea, Vietnam, and the first Gulf War combined.

The Pentagon still officially bans women from ground combat, but in Iraq female soldiers are in combat all the time. This is partly because they are serving in roles previously reserved for men and partly because the Iraq war has no front line or safe zones. Mortars come flying into base camps; grenades and bombs blow up tanks and trucks; gunfire comes out of crowds. The front line in this war is the street, and there is no hiding from it.

Yet even as women are flying helicopters, dropping bombs, raiding houses, driving tanks, acting as gunners, guarding checkpoints, and treating the wounded in the midst of battle, most civilians still think of female soldiers as either nurses or paper-pushers.

"Nobody recognizes me as a soldier. Nobody asks me to speak or go on parades," Army Captain Claudia Tascon told me. "I worked my butt off over there, I got a Bronze Star [one of the highest awards in the military], but I get no recognition.

I'm four foot eleven; I have long curly hair; I'm womanly; I wear makeup. Nobody believes I'm a soldier."

Mickiela said the same thing. "Nobody believes I was in a real war," she told me. "They won't even listen when I talk about it."

So I decided to listen, seeking out soldiers. I traveled and telephoned, meeting soldiers all over the country to interview them. It wasn't hard. Women soldiers want to tell their stories—they want to be recognized for the dangers they have endured and the sacrifices they have made. And they want the rest of us to know what it's really like to be a woman at war.

These are some of the stories I heard.

CARLYE GARCIA

When Carlye Garcia was seventeen, at the beginning of her senior year in high school, she enlisted in the Army National Guard. High school is the time when most recruits join up. Some join for patriotic reasons, but many enlist to pay for college, to get out of dead-end towns, or to escape troubled home lives. Carlye (who pronounces her name Carol) joined for the money, the challenge, and the discipline.

"I grew up in Watertown, a little town of 20,000 people in southern Wisconsin," she told me.

"My dad's a supervisor at a bakery; my mom's a bank teller. I didn't have any direction after high school, so when some guy talked to me about being in the National Guard band, I thought that sounded fun. I went to see the recruiter, and he told me one of the best paying jobs I could get as a female in the army was the military police. So that's what I joined."

This was December 2000, before the attacks of September 11 or either of the wars in Afghanistan or Iraq, so Carlye thought she had nothing to fear. Furthermore, the National Guard hadn't been sent to war since Korea in the early 1950s, so it was reasonable to assume that her job would be playing in a band, fighting forest fires, or rescuing people from floods in her home state. She had no way of knowing that the Guard would soon make up 40 percent of the soldiers in Iraq.

After she graduated from high school and turned eighteen, Carlye went to Fort Leonard Wood in Missouri to do her basic training, otherwise known as boot camp. The training was grueling and she was always being yelled at and punished, but that didn't bother her. She was pretty fit, and she considered the training only a kind of game. Then came 9/11, and the rules changed. Carlye and thousands of other National Guard recruits were about to go to war.

Carlye was nineteen by the time she arrived in Iraq. It was June 2003, four months after the war had officially begun, and she found an Iraq so crushed that most of it was nothing but rubble and dust. The air stank of burning buildings, feces, and pollution. "I saw a lot of buildings and roads blown up, a lot of abandoned tanks and trucks. Everything was deserted. Then when I got into Baghdad a couple days later, it seemed so crowded and scary. There were so many people!"

Her job was to rebuild and guard the police stations that had been bombed in the first part of the war and to train Iraqi police to work the American way, that is, without taking bribes or beating people up, she said. Every morning, she had to get up at dawn, climb into a Humvee truck with the two men who made up her team, and drive through the bomb-laden roads of Baghdad to reach a police station. The job was extremely dangerous, especially for her, because, as the lowest-ranking soldier in her team, she had to be the gunner. That meant she had to stand, holding her rifle at the ready, with the upper half of her body sticking out the roof of the Humvee, making her the most visible target on the truck.

In each police station, Carlye was given a position to guard, along with other soldiers, and would spend the next twelve hours either standing or sitting in the heat with her rifle pointed out, or searching people who came into the station. "Finally, the next squad comes, relieves you, you load up, go home, clean and put everything away, sleep, and do it over again the next day," she said.

Through it all, the heat was unbearable—Iraq summers can go up to 126 degrees Fahrenheit—especially as the soldiers had to wear full combat fatigues (those camouflage uniforms we see in photographs), helmets, and army boots, and carry up to forty pounds of equipment. At night, they slept in crowded, co-ed tents with no air-conditioning and only three feet or so between each cot. "I never got any sleep 'cause it was so hot," Carlye said. Showers were rare, and the toilets were all Porta-Johns, which stank in the desert heat.

Yet none of this bothered Carlye as much as the constant sexual harassment. It came from her fellow soldiers and from Iraqi men, who would sometimes expose themselves to her and the other women. The worst, though, was the way she was treated by her team leader and squad leader, the two men with whom she had to spend most of her time every day.

"My team leader was a very controlling, arrogant individual, and my squad leader was a pervert. They were both older, like thirty-five or forty, and they would point out Iraqi girls and say disgusting sexual stuff about them all the time. These girls were only twelve or thirteen years old! And my team leader treated me like a little kid, calling me pet names, harassing me. He wouldn't let me talk to anyone—he had really weird control issues. So I sat up in the Humvee turret alone and I never talked to anyone all day.

"I think the problem was that he had a crush on me and I'd turned him down, and that's why he kept me isolated like that. I tried to get switched, but they wouldn't do it."

Sexual harassment by male soldiers is a pervasive problem for women in the military, as is sexual assault and rape. The military has been traditionally male for so long that many men, especially the older ones, will not accept women as equals, and some of them express this through sexual attacks. Several women told me they felt in such danger from their fellow soldiers that they carried knives with them for protection. "The men only let you be three things in the military: a bitch, a ho, or a dyke," Mickiela said. "You're a bitch if you won't sleep with them, a ho if you have even one boyfriend, and a dyke also if you won't sleep with them. So you can't win whatever you do."

Some women soldiers told me they got used to the constant sexual remarks and learned to brush them off, but others said the harassment was so relentless it became unbearable. "One of the things I hated the most was when you walk into the chow hall and there's a bunch of guys who just stop eating and stare at you," Carlye said. "Every time you bent down, somebody would say something. It got to the point where I was afraid to walk past certain people 'cause I didn't want to hear their comments. It really wears you down."

One of the worst consequences of sexual harassment is that it makes the women unable to trust their own comrades—and trust and love between soldiers is the only comfort they can find at war. "I didn't trust anybody in my company after a few months," Carlye said. "I saw so many girls get screwed over from the sexual harassment. I didn't trust anybody and I still don't."

Between the harassment from the soldiers on her own side and the increasing hostility from the Iraqis as the war went on, Carlye began to hate every minute of her time in Iraq. "I was counting the days by then—it seemed to be taking forever. I just wanted to go home. I had a sinking feeling each time I woke up."

Then, one day, while she was riding in her Humvee up in her gunner's turret, a roadside bomb exploded beside her.

"I must have passed out, because when I woke up, I was in the truck by myself. My ears were ringing, and my whole body hurt really bad. But it didn't faze me much—I just thought, OK, I'm alive. I hated it over there, so I was kind of pissed that I didn't get hurt worse so I could go home."

Carlye downplays her wounds when she talks about being blown up, but Laura Naylor, another soldier I interviewed and a friend of Carlye, happened to be in the same convoy and saw the whole thing. "Carlye was in a Humvee behind us, and the roadside bomb went off right next to it. It totally destroyed her weapon—the shrapnel just sawed off its tip. She was pushed inside the Humvee by the explosion, and the shrapnel cut up her face and her arm. They thought that she'd broken her arm in two spots, but it was just shrapnel sticking out. When she was unconscious and we thought we'd lost her—that was probably one of my scariest moments. I just can't imagine losing someone like that, who I've grown to know and love and trust over the deployment."

Carlye was sent to the first-aid station, where the shrapnel was removed from her face. "You can see scars but it's not hideous," she told me. "And my eardrums were ruptured. I went back to our base and I couldn't work for a month because I couldn't hear anything. Now I have constant tinnitus—ringing in the ears—it's annoying. My hearing's not as good as it was, but it's OK."

In July 2004, Carlye went home, and three weeks later began to attend college. Gradually, however, she found herself growing increasingly jumpy, irritable, and antisocial: the pyschological reaction to war often takes time to hit. She finally sought counseling, which she says helped. Now that nearly two years have passed since she came back, I asked her what she considers the worst and best parts of her time in Iraq.

"The best part is that now I have a drive to

succeed," she said. Then she hesitated and added, "But I hated it—I can't think of a best part. Maybe the camaraderie, the friendships I made. But every day there was a bad day."

LAURA NAYLOR

Carlye's friend Laura, who is also from Wisconsin, enlisted in March 2001 when she was nineteen, six months before September 11. "I had no idea war was ahead," she told me. "I was walking home from class one day my freshman year at college, and I realized I didn't want to go home for the summer and I couldn't really afford to stay in Madison, where I was living, because I was paying for my own education. So, I decided to join the National Guard. Why not? One weekend a month and two weeks in the summer and my whole education paid for—it sounded great. Plus, I love adventure, I'm patriotic, and I love a challenge, so it was really appealing to me."

Like Carlye, Laura chose the military police because it offered the largest bonus—$8,000 versus the usual $5,000 offered at the time to National Guard recruits—and seemed the most exciting. "They said that my company was highly deployable, but at the time I signed up, they were doing a peace mission in Nicaragua and then Hungary, and it wasn't anything to be afraid of because there was no war. I thought it would be a great opportunity to see the world, even if I did get pulled out of school a little while. Plus I consider myself a really tough chick, so I thought I could handle it."

She did get pulled out of school, during her junior year of college, in March 2003. By July, she was in Baghdad.

For the first month of her deployment, Laura felt proud of what America was doing. "I actually wrote a letter to the editor saying I could see good happening and I was really proud that we could give people freedom. But that changed through the time I was there." I asked her why.

"Well, at first the kids would come out and cheer us—everyone would give us thumbs-up and yell, 'Good America!' and it was a really positive atmosphere because you could see that these people loved their freedom. However, within the fourteen months we were there, it kept getting worse and worse. The insurgency was growing exponentially, they were getting sick of our occupation, people were dying, things weren't getting better, and by the time we left, the kids were throwing rocks at us all the time, they're giving us the middle finger, there was anti-American graffiti everywhere. We went from helping the Iraqis as much as possible to literally only securing ourselves. All our missions were based on how do we survive instead of how do we help the Iraqis survive."

Laura told a story to illustrate how Iraqi

distrust of Americans was growing. "The third day we got to our police station, we got shot at by two insurgents and we shot back, and we killed one of the insurgents and three civilians. Well, those three civilian families turned against us and had all their friends and family turn against us, so you can see how the insurgency would just grow every day. Every time there was a collision with the insurgents, we might kill a civilian and those people would turn against us as well.

"Then, on October 27 of 2003, the police station where we had worked for three months was destroyed by a car bomb, killing twenty-one people, five of whom were Iraqi police officers and the rest civilians. That was the worst moment for me. We'd gotten to know the police officers and the kids in the neighborhood really well, and when the police station was destroyed, I watched those same kids being dragged out of the building completely charred and burned and dead. That made me really step back and say, what are we doing here and is this even worth it?"

Laura was sent home for a two-week break in January 2004. "At that point we were still told that we were going to be home in April, so I expected just four more months. We ended up getting extended about five times, and we didn't get home till sixteen months after we started." Her experience was typical. Because the Iraq War is being fought entirely by volunteer soldiers, and because it has turned out to be longer, more difficult, violent, and expensive than President Bush's government had foreseen, the Pentagon has been making soldiers stay much longer than it promised and sending soldiers back to fight again, two, three and even more times, even when they have been wounded or traumatized.

As the months wore on, the war became increasingly dangerous. "Every night, mortars were landing in our compound," Laura said. "One day I went to the portable toilet and just after I left, we were barraged by mortars and that exact toilet was completely gone. You couldn't even tell it had been there. At night we were mortared all the time. A tent near mine was completely destroyed. And you wonder, 'My God, this could have happened to me.' That's a constant thought in your head. Then out on the road, we had IEDs [improvised explosive devices, or homemade bombs] all the time. We had thirty-five Purple Hearts in our company because we worked in the most dangerous districts of Baghdad, and we were driving for hours every day, waiting for an IED to blow up around us."

An IED is what wounded Carlye. It was also what killed one of Laura's best friends, Michelle Witmer, who was only twenty when she died. I asked Laura how she coped with seeing her friends killed and wounded around her.

"You just have to," she said sadly. "It's survival instinct. And I would always think about my family. I'm a firm believer in God and I would console myself and think this is God's plan, this is something He planned for my life, so be it."

Once Laura had finally gone home for good, she felt all right for the first year. "But then I went to sergeant school in August of 2005, and I ended up having panic attacks. I had late-onset PTSD [post-traumatic stress disorder], which took over my life in the fall. I couldn't concentrate. I was in school but I would start crying in the middle of nowhere. I couldn't take loud noises or heavy metal music—I would freak out. My blood pressure was through the roof and I was depressed and stressed, and for the first time in my entire life I did not have control over my emotions or my well-being. I couldn't haul myself out of this slump I was in. It was the scariest thing.

"So I talked to a therapist, who was wonderful, and I got on medication, just a small dose, but enough to settle my anxiety and depression levels. I'm tons better now. I can actually watch fireworks without freaking out, and I can hear a loud noise without wanting to crawl underneath the table."

Laura has stayed close to Carlye and other women she served with, and also gives presentations about the war to local community groups, which she finds therapeutic. But she says she will never forget the soldiers like Michelle, who died in Iraq, or those little Iraqi girls who were burned to death by a bomb.

CLAUDIA TASCON

If Claudia Tascon had been in Baghdad with Laura, she might well have been called to help those Iraqi children, for Claudia served with a medical corps in Iraq. As a result, she has a more positive attitude about the war than do Carlye or Laura.

"Because I'm more in the curing business than the killing business, I've seen the good of what we've done," she said. "I have my thoughts but never say them aloud because I saw the good stuff. We had dentists and doctors put themselves in harm's way to help kids in villages or bring them home to cure them. I can't say anything bad about the war."

Claudia immigrated to the United States from Colombia when she was thirteen, learned English in a year, and grew up in Elmer, New Jersey, where her parents bought and ran a cleaning business. Her fascination with the military began in high school. "I wanted to be a doctor. Then I saw a movie about army doctors and I thought it looked great and fun to get to shoot guns and still work in medicine." She went to college at the University of Massachusetts, where she joined the ROTC so she could become an officer. At the age of twenty, she enlisted in the New Jersey National Guard. "I joined in 1997 and I thought I'd be in charge of natural disasters in the state. I never thought I'd go to Iraq.

"I probably wouldn't have joined if I knew that I'd go to war. I just wanted the experience. And it's been great for me. In the civilian world, you'd never have a twenty-three-year-old in charge of millions of dollars of supplies, like I was, or in charge of people's lives. It teaches you to have strength. It's been a great experience, even at war."

Claudia had risen to first lieutenant by the time she was sent to Iraq in December 2004, where she was put in charge of a warehouse full of medical supplies and had eight soldiers under her command. One of her challenges was getting the men to obey her. "Some men tend to not like it when women tell them what to do. I had confrontations with a couple of my sergeants. But we worked it out."

Her time at war was spent organizing the warehouse and helping the sick and wounded. "We'd fly out to villages in helicopters and cure young kids, and supply medical units and infantry medics all over northern Iraq with medical tools." She also worked out a way to find medical supplies for the Iraqi army, which won her the Bronze Star. "The Iraqis were the ones getting blown up and wounded the most, they were the targets, but all they had for wounds was saline solution."

Claudia was stationed in Tikrit, Saddam Hussein's hometown, in the volatile Sunni triangle, and her base was bombed all the time. "A lot of the people who bombed us weren't Iraqis; they were from other countries," she said. "I got to know some Iraqis because they set up a storage area for me, and they were just normal people trying to make a living. They just needed money to feed their families."

Aside from the reluctance of some men to obey her commands, Claudia didn't have as much trouble with sexual harassment as do many female soldiers. She attributed this to being in a medical unit, which had a more equal balance of women to men than most other units, to being an officer, and to having women as friends.

"I didn't feel isolated because there were a lot of other women where I was. The ratio of men to women was about sixty to thirty-five or so. In my unit there were a few female officers too, although less in my battalion—maybe two or three out of thirty. But we women roomed together, took care of each other, walked in the dark together. We were buddies."

Claudia is thirty now. She never became a doctor, but works as a chemist and evaluator in a fragrance factory in New Jersey. She hopes to marry and have children. I asked her what she would do if she were called back to Iraq.

"If I was sent back, I wouldn't want to go. It's not that I'm nervous—I've done it; I know the job. It's having to come back to civilian life again. Two years of my life were taken out, I became a different person, and it took a long time to get back. It's tough to adjust from working at top speed to being normal again. It's like going from living your life at ten billion miles an hour to ten miles an hour. And there I was a boss and here I'm not.

"If I did get redeployed, though, I would go. You develop camaraderie in the Army, a sense of responsibility for other people, especially when you're in a leadership role. For me to leave the army when my soldiers would have to go to war without me—I couldn't live with that."

LYDIA SANCHEZ

Lydia grew up in a small city near Los Angeles, California, a third-generation Mexican and the eldest of five girls. In late 2000, when she was in high school, she joined the Marine Corps Reserves, lured in by the glamorous image of the marines and a friend who had joined. "My parents were getting divorced, so I thought I could join the Reserves and come home when the fighting and divorce was over. Plus their money was tied up in court stuff, so there was none left for college. This was before 9/11. If it had been after, I never would have joined."

The recruiter who signed her up lied to her. "He told me I had six or seven jobs to choose from—females don't get to do everything—so I chose firefighting. I thought that would be exciting. But at the end of boot camp I was told the position I was training for was only for a man. So I had to do embarkation and logistics." That meant loading up airplanes and ordering supplies.

Her recruiter also promised Lydia that she would get full benefits for school. "But it wasn't true," she said. "I only got partial benefits because I wasn't on active duty. I got about $250 a month. It barely paid for one class."

Lying recruiters have become a big problem for the military. In May 2005, the army reported that the number of cases of "inappropriate actions" on the part of recruiters had jumped by over 60 percent since 1999. Recruiters were telling high school students that the war was over, helping them forge diplomas and cheat on drug tests, and threatening to arrest them if they failed to show up at recruitment stations.[1]

Lydia trained at the Marine Corps Recruit Depot in Parris Island, South Carolina, where she spent three months and a week. "The first month they really try to break you down. Everything is very difficult. You lose all sense of time. They don't tell you what's going on, and they yell insults at you all the time. And there was some pushing. The time I got pushed, I wanted to push back, but I didn't. I knew you couldn't. One drill instructor got in trouble for breaking a guy's hand.

"The sergeants also make you join in bullying certain people; that's one of their methods. This one woman kept peeing in her bed at night, and they told her she was disgusting and made her get up early to clean her bed. She told me she'd never had that problem before. It turned out she had a severe bladder infection and it got to the point where she lost control of her bladder at night."

Lydia adjusted eventually, and made it through basic training all right. But not everyone did—thirty out of the seventy women who started flunked out. "They either hurt themselves, failed the running test, or couldn't handle it mentally," she said. Ten of the men flunked out too. One of the toughest aspects of boot camp is that if you miss even one day because of injury or illness, you have to start the whole program from the beginning. This threat makes some people crack up. Mickiela said three women in her boot camp tried to commit suicide.

"I had the most excruciating pain at one point in my legs," Lydia said. "But if I complained, I knew I'd be stuck there and have to retrain from the start. Now I have issues with my legs 'cause I ignored the pain and kept going."

Lydia graduated from boot camp in April 2001, becoming one of the small 6 percent of marines who are female, went home for ten days, then took her marine combat training in North Carolina for another month. There, along with seventy-five other men and women, she learned how to shoot an M-16, dig a foxhole, build a tent, and go on night patrols. "None of this was right for Iraq," she said. "We were in a forest, not sand."

Like Carlye, Lydia had to endure a lot of sexual harassment, both during training and at war. "My first experience of it was right after combat training. A male marine was spying on the women's quarters from an electrical piping duct in the building. But mostly it was the senior people, the high-ranking people, who were doing it, not my peers. The major in my shop invited me for drinks at his hotel. I was shocked because they aren't allowed to do that, but I'm sure he was thinking if I said anything, nobody would believe me. They'd believe him over me. So I had to keep it to myself." She was right. Most female soldiers don't report sexual harassment or assault because they will either not be believed or will be considered traitors by their comrades. Furthermore, they are supposed to report their assaults to their superiors, even though those superiors may be the very men who attacked them.

After her training was finished, Lydia went home, enrolled in school, and worked in a bank. She was home during 9/11, but still didn't expect to go to war. Then she was called up in November 2003. "I didn't want to go, I didn't want to leave my family. People were dying. Marines were drowning as they were crossing rivers; airplanes were being shot down. I was terrified. I'm close to my family and they felt the same."

On January 6, 2004, her unit was activated. "At first I didn't understand why we were going. They'd looked for a year and hadn't found any bombs. It was getting old for a lot of people— enough is enough."

I asked her if she had believed that there was a connection between Osama bin Laden and Iraq, as so many Americans had early in the war.

"No. I took a couple of classes and the professors explained that bin Laden had nothing to do with Iraq."

In early March 2004, Lydia was flown into Iraq. Once she settled into her base just above Fallujah, the sexual harassment began again. Only this time, it came from a sergeant, her direct boss.

"He made my life hell. He was always making sexual remarks to me and trying to get me alone. Once he said, 'You look good in glasses. I've always had a thing for Hispanic women in glasses.' I didn't even know how to reply. He was thirty-eight, and I was twenty-two. He was a white guy. He kept making everyone else leave on a job and keeping me behind. I'd ask my friends not to leave me alone with him, but he'd order them to go. I had to tell another female about him in the end, even though I didn't want to cause trouble, but he was so awful to me that I couldn't live right."

Once Lydia rejected her sergeant, he began to take revenge, just as Carlye's team leader had.

"He'd put me on a twelve-hour day shift and then on a twelve-hour night shift with no sleep. I'd ask to sleep for an hour, and he wouldn't let me. We were working nonstop, too. He did that four or five times. Finally, other superiors saw it and stopped it. They told him he couldn't be on my shift anymore. He came to apologize and said, 'I never knew I was making you uncomfortable.' I didn't believe him."

Meanwhile, Lydia's base was being constantly bombarded with rockets and mortars. "About five times it was really big and bad, where the attacks lasted five minutes or more and people were hurt and killed. But every day we'd hear something, a big blast or boom." Aside from a ring of sandbags around the camp, the soldiers had no protection. They slept in canvas tents, and all they could do when they heard incoming bombs was put on their helmets and flak jackets and hit the floor.

One evening a new female soldier came in, and Lydia helped her set up her cot in their tent. The next morning, the new soldier went for a jog on the main road. "There was a mortar attack and shrapnel tore off her bicep completely. She was bleeding everywhere. Another time, one of our pilots was shot in the neck and killed in the air. A couple of people I worked with from another unit died, too. One was killed on patrol. I didn't know him well but I worked with him every day."

Lydia felt in danger all the time. "Every time you heard something, you had to duck and look at your watch, because our side would detonate any IEDs they found every hour on the hour. Everything else in between was an attack."

Between the attacks and the heat, she soon stopped being able to sleep, even though she was exhausted. "I found myself drinking NyQuil every night. I lost a lot of weight. I couldn't eat—I was too nervous, there was no time, I was always working, it was hot. I would choose to sleep over eating. When I came home, my family said, 'What happened to you?'

"Now I get terrible headaches—so bad I can't move. I never had that before Iraq."

Unlike Carlye and Laura, Lydia spent most of her time in Iraq on base, and except when the base was under attack, her days were dull. She would rise every morning at four-thirty, clean up, fix the constantly collapsing tents, and do office work until evening. Though she was promoted to corporal, the routine never changed. Her experience was typical of life for most soldiers in any war: boredom, interrupted by spells of chaos and terror.

Her tour ended in late September 2005, and she flew back home with relief. I asked her what she thinks about the war now.

"I think we need to bring everybody back. It's awful. We've done what we can do. Our people are dying; their people are dying. We've spent so much money—the Iraqis don't want us there."

And the other marines she knows—how do they feel?

"We feel this war is done."

NOTE
1. *Army Recruiting*. PBS NewsHour. May 12, 2005. www.pbs.org/newshour/bb/military/jan-june05/recruiting_5-12.htm.

WORDSMITH AT WAR

a miliblog by Lee Kelley

Captain Lee Kelley was deployed to the Anbar Province of Iraq from 2005 to 2006. Since then, he has ended his military service. He is now a single dad living in Salt Lake City, Utah, with his two children. He is busy at work on a nonfiction book about his experiences in Iraq, as well as his first novel. His writing from Iraq has attracted the attention of National Public Radio, Time magazine, and other media. His miliblog, http://www.wordsmithatwar.blogcity.com/, contains more of his writing from Iraq.

The Government Center—March 4, 2006

A couple of days ago I went to the government center in downtown Ramadi. This is where the governor has his office, and the local tribal leaders and sheiks meet and do business. I drove down with my battalion commander, Lieutenant Colonel M (the boss), and his PSD (personal security detail), which consists of Sergeant C and Specialist T. I didn't necessarily have a mission down there, but the boss had been telling me I should come down with him sometime, for the experience of seeing the local government at work. I called and asked if he had an extra seat this day. He did.

We did a convoy brief, then geared up and loaded the vehicle around 1000. Once we were all in the vehicle, the boss looked over at the driver,

Specialist T, and the gunner, Sergeant C, and asked, "Whose turn is it to pray?" He did not ask, "Does someone want to say a prayer?" This was simply a given. They never left on a mission without a prayer. Specialist T immediately said a prayer that was quick, tailored to our mission, and humble. I liked that. It's a good way to begin a mission. It made me proud of them.

We linked up with another security element at the detention facility, where we picked up a detainee who had been "cleared" by the governor of Ramadi. Apparently they went to college together. The governor knew his family and vouched for him. Our mission was to bring him down to the governor for a release, and also for another meeting with local leaders. We stopped for a minute at the gate to load our weapons, because once we were off the FOB (forward operating base), we entered a different world. No longer are you surrounded by layers of security. You are now in the red zone, not the green zone, and any atrocity or act of violence has to be expected. Ramadi, Iraq, is a city of half a million people who have been through a hell of a lot. First it was Saddam, and now years of being caught up in the crossfire, as it were, of that proverbial old battle between the good and bad guys. Change does not always come easily, and the citizens of Ramadi have been through many growing pains. And none of this even begins to touch upon the historical and religious implications of what they've experienced down through the generations. Ramadi has certainly been a nucleus of insurgent activity, but it's getting better. We are dissecting.

I'm sitting in the backseat of a fully armored HMMWV (high-mobility multipurpose wheeled vehicle), peering out at the world through thick bulletproof glass, scanning down countless alleys and on rooftops for anyone with a weapon, or anything that looks like a threat. By weapons I mean RPGs, grenades, AK-47s, land mines, suicide-vehicle IEDs—you name it and it's possible in Ramadi. I see children playing, adults standing around, and women walking down streets in groups of two or three. Most people watch us as we pass, a convoy of armored vehicles flying down the streets aggressively. Sergeant C is on full alert. Having the best vantage point as gunner, he's constantly readjusting his position as Specialist T steers around obstacles. Out on the interstates, civilian vehicles see a military convoy coming through and they know to pull off on the shoulder, giving you a wide berth. But downtown, the streets are narrower, and there are more obstacles. When you approach intersections, the lead vehicle sounds a siren and the gunners motion with their weapons for vehicles to make way. But sometimes you drive within feet of the locals. And you hope that the driver in one of them is not suicidal.

You have to go around big potholes and chunks

of concrete blocking part of the lane. It's not a good feeling, because all your training tells you that these are ideal sites for IEDs. In fact, as we drive past some of them, the boss and Specialist T point out things like, "Oh yeah, this is where so-and-so hit the IED last week," or "Where was that suicide vehicle IED attack the other day? Yep, we just passed it." The threat is very real, and you can sense it in the air. You can't think, "it won't happen to us." You have to assume it will. Yet we discuss it in the same tone we might talk about last night's football game.

Most of the buildings look like run-down apartment complexes, with rugs and clothing hanging from the balconies. Every empty window looks dangerous; every blind alley seems a threat. And down those alleys, you see the dirty and littered streets where people live and fight for their lives under the scrutiny of this unforgiving desert sun. The closer you get to the heart of the city, the more cramped become the conditions in which the people of Ramadi appear to live. When you get near the government center, you feel like you're in bombed-out Beirut. I've never been to Beirut, but from what I've seen on TV and books I've read, this has got to be the closest thing to it in Iraq. For blocks around the center, the buildings are riddled with bullet holes from countless firefights between coalition forces and insurgents. You see the side of a yellow building, for example, and the entire three-story space of it has two-inch to twelve-inch spots of bare concrete from bullets, almost like some artist's ghastly rendition of living art. Huge chunks of buildings are gone, and others have collapsed in on themselves. There are soldiers and marines manning towers and positions that are some of the deadliest in the world, much less in Iraq. Once there, I'm told by the boss and the guys that we need to run from the vehicle to the door with weapons at the ready, because there are a lot of snipers and mortar attacks down there. And so I ran. Inside there are around a hundred Iraqi men who are all somehow affiliated with the local government or trying to participate in the process. Some wear jeans and T-shirts and smile at you. Others wear elaborate headscarves, man-dresses, and sandals and simply stare at you mysteriously as they walk past. We bring the detainee inside and wait for the governor's arrival. We exchange nods and smiles. We greet them in Arabic.

I'm led into a large conference room with a twenty-foot table spanning the middle. There are Army and Marine officers standing around in conversation with Iraqi men, as if they were getting ready for a corporate meeting in a skyscraper in downtown New York City. They seem casual— cool, calm, and collected. Their body armor and weapons are stacked on a chair. They're doing the grin and grab, the old handshake polka. But if you inspect further, you will notice that for every senior officer in the meeting room, there are probably three or four heavily armed soldiers or marines, completely alert and always aware of their surroundings. They're lurking around the room, standing in hallways, scanning the parking lot. Weapons are loaded, and it takes only your thumb flipping a little switch to change your worldview from safe to semiautomatic.

The governor's office, while perhaps a little tacky by American standards, is pretty imposing. It's a fifty-foot room with a massive wooden desk. Along both sides of the room are ornate gold-colored sofas with gold cushions. There are nice little glass tables in front of them with ashtrays sitting on beaded cup holders. The curtains are also gold. There are some fake flower arrangements and a small TV. The huge rug dominating the floor has many colors but is laced with gold. Behind the governor's desk there is an Iraqi flag, a small grandfather clock, and some books. We hear a small commotion, and realize the big man himself has entered the building. The governor arrives, and there are some formalities as Lieutenant Colonel M works with some Iraqi men to have the release paperwork signed and filled out properly. Once it's over, hands are shaken all around and the newly freed detainee seems all too happy.

After the governor's meeting is over, we run across the parking lot into another door farther down the building, to visit a man I'll call Mr. H. Mr. H is the guy who sets up meetings between the government, the Americans, and the tribal leaders and sheiks. He also has a big room, though not as ornate as the governor's. He sits on one side, on a large couch, motioning for us to make ourselves comfortable. The boss, Captain G, our interpreter, and I sit across from Mr. H. Again, we take off our body armor and place our weapons on the couch next to us. There's no need to wear them right then. We're sitting with a colleague having a cordial meeting. Yes, we're literally in the heart of the lion's den, but there are others securing the building. And they're good at what they do. Our purpose is more political, less combative for the next hour or so. Besides, Specialist T and Sergeant C are out in the hallway, keeping an eye on things.

Lieutenant Colonel M begins by asking how Mr. H's children and family are doing. Friendly small talk ensues for a few minutes. Mr. H thanks us for all the school supplies we've provided the local children. He says his own son came home with some and was quite excited about it. Mr. H looks about fifty, has very kind eyes, and wears a light green suit with a tan shirt. His shoes are black leather. As he talks, he holds his silver glasses in his hand or unconsciously folds a single piece of white paper into squares. They discuss the future of Ramadi, the recent mosque bombings in Baghdad, the weather, and some other subjects that I cannot address here. During the talks, one of Mr. H's assistants brings in a few glasses and some bottled water. He places them on the little glass tables. We thank him. Mr. H seems very appreciative to have the opportunity to sit and talk like this. Mr. H tells us, through the interpreter, that he had a dream about Lieutenant Colonel M and Lieutenant Colonel Mac (who was recently killed). They were all at Baghdad International Airport together, and they were trying to get Mr. H to fly to America with them. We all had a good laugh about that.

The boss and Captain G have the air of men who are visiting a friend they see all the time, and I guess they do. They've built a relationship with Mr. H and others in this city, and it's exactly these kinds of relationships that are going to tip the scales for Iraq. Lieutenant Colonel Mac knew Mr. H quite well before he was killed. When Americans with good hearts and a just cause work hand-in-hand with the same type of Iraqis, the possibilities are limitless. At one point, Mr. H's eyes seemed a little wet, when he told us that he hates all the violence and he prays for Lieutenant Colonel M and his soldiers, that we can all get home safely. We eventually said our good-byes. As I approached the door, Mr. H was standing near it. I stopped and motioned for him to go first, out of respect. He put his hand over his heart, smiled, and waved me through.

A few minutes later, we were saddled up again for the ride back to the FOB. We were the third vehicle in the convoy. We had to go out of a gate and make a sharp left before we could pick up speed. As we exit the gate, an RPG was fired at the vehicle right in front of us. I had my earplugs in. I didn't even realize it was an RPG, it all happened so fast. All I heard was a muted thump, and then I felt the tension as Specialist T sped up, and Sergeant C swung his machine gun around. The gunner in the nearest vehicle started yelling, "I've got PID, I've got PID." This means positive identification, not unlike police talk—he had spotted the shooter. As Specialist T accelerates, we hear the unmistakable sound of a machine gun firing at the enemy. This time we didn't get him. He got away in the never-ending alleyways of Ramadi.

Less than a half hour later, we were sitting around a table in the chow hall talking and laughing about the whole thing. Not laughing in a childish, giddy way, but as men do when they live in a combat zone for prolonged periods. I don't want to be overdramatic. People see a lot worse than this every single day. But in a philosophical sense, I couldn't stop dwelling on the fact that a man put a rocket-propelled grenade on his shoulder, aimed, and fired, and the thing exploded within fifty feet of our vehicle. We were the objects he saw through the sight on his weapon as he squinted with one eye and placed his shaky finger on the trigger. I'm just thankful nobody was hurt.

I am humbled by so many soldiers and marines I work with out here. These men and women are truly incredible. But sometimes it's the young kids that really impress me. For some reason, young twenty-somethings like Specialist T and Sergeant C just amaze me with their professionalism, their upstanding attitudes, and their ability to live in this environment every day and deal with it so well. Age does not better prepare you for war, necessarily, but it perhaps gives you more life experience from which to draw strength when the going gets tough. These guys sit around the chow hall after an RPG comes so close and smile, let the adrenaline subside. It's a good feeling, to be surrounded by folks with the wisdom to pray before a mission like this but the mental agility to laugh amiably when it's over.

> *What lies behind us and what lies before us are tiny matters compared to what lies within us.*
> —William Morrow

Praying Together—September 5, 2005

We pray together a lot here.

And in those quiet moments I've come to realize something about myself. More than ever before in my life, I believe that doing good works in the service of others is the noblest cause. Soldiering is one profession that exemplifies this concept well.

Someone once said, "Military officers are professionals in the art of controlling chaos and violence." And I think this is true to an extent. But we are also expert at leading people in the service of others. Armies do not go to war simply because the soldiers opt to. They go to war because the leaders of a country, who were elected by the people, decide that war is necessary and unavoidable.

In this same light, there have been some tragedies in the world of late that sadden me deeply. Recently in Iraq, a few thousand people were walking across a bridge near Baghdad in a religious procession. Someone yelled, "Suicide bomber!" or there was somehow brought upon them the fear of a suicide bomber, and a stampede broke out. People were crushed, and the railings on the bridge broke, causing people to fall into the water. More than eight hundred people, mostly women and children, perished. How sad a thing to occur. What a sordid state of affairs.

And then there's the recent disaster in New Orleans. I spent the first twenty years of my life in that city. Since I joined the army, except for a few sparse periods of time, I have never called it my home again. But I have family there, and many people whom I care about deeply. I also have many memories, which come rushing back on me as I watch the floodwaters on the news.

This is a somber note tonight, my friends, but I've been feeling a bit frustrated and helpless lately. I know that my immediate family is OK, but there are countless extended family members and friends who I can only pray escaped harm. My parents do not know if their car, their truck, their home, or their possessions are still where they left them.

I am not a religious man, in the sense of having one religion I can call my own. I was raised Catholic, but in my teenage years I developed some theological problems with the religion as a whole. Having said this, I pray often, and know that there is a God and that I live an inspired life.

Catholic, Muslim, Buddhist, Mormon, Presbyterian, Jewish, Baptist, Wiccan. I say, hey, whatever gets you through the night, because I believe that in the end we are our own judges, and we have to deal with the things we've done, or failed to do. I have an extensive library back home, and on the shelves of that library reside almost every Bible. I have spent time reading through those books over the years. I find them all compelling. I simply cannot pick just one.

Merriam-Webster's definition of *eclectic* is (1) selecting what appears to be best in various doctrines, methods, or styles; (2) composed of elements drawn from various sources.

This is the way I have approached my religion. I follow my heart and my instinct, which I believe are the parts of me that are closest to God. I have fundamental and categorical problems with certain parts of some religions, while other teachings of those same faiths really hit home and touch me as truth.

I still have my original dog tags from 1992, and they list my name, Social Security number, blood type, and religious preference. Some people put *no preference*. In my case, that would be inaccurate. If anything, I have too many preferences. So my dog tags say *eclectic*. I'll admit that when I did it, I was twenty years old and thought I was kind of turning my nose up at authority for daring to be different. *Eclectic* was not really a choice, but I told them anyway, and they made the dog tags.

Over the years I'd forgotten about it. You do not look at your dog tags every day and read them. But I like them very much now, because instead of a religion, I basically have an adjective on my dog tags. And it's an adjective that describes my musical tastes, my religious beliefs, my choice of books, and my life. I've traveled a lot in my thirty-three years. I've lived a lot of places, and I've known many people whose faces I don't easily forget.

As I've said, I am not a religious man. But I still like the fact that I am here in Iraq with this unit, and that we pray together often. We pray at every meeting, and before a mission. Prayer means many different things to people, but at the core it is a gathering of will, a summoning of the spirit toward a higher power, for help, for guidance, for support, for strength.

Do me a favor, will you? Regardless of your

religion, or lack thereof, pray for the people of Iraq, and that we can soften the hearts of the insurgents. Pray for the people of New Orleans. And pray for us too, as we are always praying for you.

> *Life is the art of drawing without an eraser.*
>
> —John Gardner

Fire in the Night—October 3, 2005

We burn a lot of things out here.

There is a huge pit where we burn our trash. There is no city dump to drop things off at, where trash is divided into papers, plastics, and metals to help with the ever-imminent energy crisis always lurking behind the door.

There is also no Environmental Protection Agency.

Just tonight I walked outside and the air was thick with acrid smoke. It smelled like burning plastic or rubber or something else one wouldn't normally burn back home.

We burn anything that may be considered classified. It could be the address label off of a box that our family sent us, or an official military document. If the enemy can use it to his advantage, just burn it. Leave nothing to chance.

There are burn barrels and little pits dug into

the ground all over. Sometimes at night you pass by an area and see mysterious darkened figures around a barrel alight with orange flame, like hobos in a New York back alley.

Add this to the Muslim prayers coming over loudspeakers from way too close, and you have the makings of a scene from *The Twilight Zone*. The man who is usually praying sounds passionate, and fully enthralled in the words. It reminds me of a Native American prayer, as the vibrato voice rises and falls with a rhythm that is strange and unsettling.

I think Alfred Hitchcock would have loved this place at night. Without streetlamps, the darkness is complete here. And now that it's daylight saving time, you can find yourself on the walk back from the chow hall after dinner in a strange land of shadow and danger, your perception limited to the power of your flashlight. Fire breaks up the darkness.

As the weeks roll by, I fill up a box with paper I need to burn. I like to go out at night under the stars when I think it's safe and feed my paper into the fire, piece by piece. My eyes dance with the flames as my thoughts are reflected in them.

I stand close because the heat doesn't bother me much. I have become accustomed to heat. Never again will I complain about the temperature in the summer in America. Conversely, 60 degrees will probably chill me to the bone.

We live our days in a place of harsh realities, of danger, of intense heat, of learning the hard way, of brotherhood, of war, of sacrifice, of bold action, of bitter tears, of love, of hate, of regeneration, and of history.

But every once in a while, in the silence of the night, we simply stand around a fire and feed paper into the flames, each one of us lost in our own thoughts.

As September came to a close, I ripped the month off my calendar and walked out to the barrel.

I felt symbolic as I sacrificed September to the fire—but it's only paper. Some of us have sacrificed much, much more.

We Support You—August 31, 2005

When you're in Iraq, mail becomes paramount.

No longer do you grab the stuff in your mailbox with the monotony that consumes you after years and years of junk mail and coupons you'll never use. The walk to the mailbox is not a mechanical part of your day anymore. No more is your mail a constant trickle of companies reminding you that you owe them money. Mail becomes a miniature Christmas, a small token or package or gift from a magical land far away that now seems kind of fuzzy in your memory, like Santa and his reindeer through the glass of a child's globe that has just been shaken and presents you with a snowy winterscape. A quickening of the spirit occurs when you receive a letter or package from your friends or family back in the United States. It must be the way a man feels receiving a message in a bottle after being shipwrecked on an island for years. This simile may be a stretch, but you get my drift.

Whether you are a true patriot and you bleed red, white, and blue or you are simply here because duty came knocking at your door and you have some honor and some pride in what you do, it feels really good to receive thoughts and prayers from all of you back home.

You may be cooking one of us some home-made brownies this morning in a snug little town in the Blue Ridge Mountains of North Carolina as you sip your Colombian coffee and enjoy watching the fog rise up off the slopes through your window, thinking about your son or daughter who is deployed in the Middle East.

You may send a photo of yourself snowboarding at the Canyons in Park City, Utah, and write "I missed you on the lift tonight," or some other inside joke in black marker right across the mountainous scene in the background to your friend in Iraq.

You may be retired. You may be a veteran. You may have been sitting in your living room just today writing a letter of appreciation on your favorite stationery and licking the seal and sending it to one of your grandchildren over here.

You may be the guy in Detroit who recently sent one of my sergeants some new boots and a carton of smokes. He signed up on www.operationac.com to sponsor a soldier deployed overseas.

You may be a child, writing a letter in first period to a soldier from your hometown. We love the flags that you draw us in crayon or marker, coloring so carefully inside the lines. And we enjoy the intelligent letters you send us, wondering what it is like over here and if we are scared.

Whoever you are, and regardless of your political interests or your feelings about the military or war or violence or our commander in chief, or Iraq, or Muslims, or the current stock market trends, we appreciate your support. Regardless of your favorite color, your skin color, the type of car you drive, your age, the college you went to, your lack of education, or your bad attitude toward teenagers and video games, we still thank you.

Because we *are* you. We are the American people, temporarily displaced for a spell in the Middle East. We exemplify virtually every race, class, profession, and opinion that you do over there across the pond. We're just fighting right now—that's all. We've been pulled away from "normal" life to serve our country as millions have done for America in past conflicts. Some of us believe in the political machines that nudge entire nations into war, and some of us just believe in ourselves and each other and doing the duty we raised our hand and swore to do.

Few know what fate waited for us behind that oath, but it took a special kind of person to make it either way.

We love our country with its high desert and thick forests, and coffee shops and bars and churches and fairs and malls and movie theaters and racetracks and bookstores and libraries and universities and quiet suburbia—a cul-de-sac streetlamp paradise, and football and Lollapalooza and children going down slides at countless parks, and tattoo parlors and motorbikes and radio stations and cell phones and Thanksgiving and days off and fast food and sensible salads and backwoods and small towns and big-city lights and Montana and Utah and New Orleans and Pennsylvania and the Midwest and the Southwest and the Pacific coast and the Great Lakes and *A Prairie Home Companion* and Seattle and Texas and New York and watching our children take their first step, or hearing them say their first word, and shopping at Wal-Mart and Best Buy and Barnes & Noble and Starbucks and driving down winding roads, and our car stereos, and barbecues and beer and our comfortable beds and the hugs of those we love and the spontaneous smiles of those we miss and, believe me, I could go on and on. We listen to a lot of music over here and that music becomes the soundtrack of our lives. Country music, religious music, soft rock, heavy metal, rap, classic rock—we listen to it all, and it inspires.

You see—we don't ever forget. In fact, all we do is work over here, and remember. So please, don't let the media fool you. We are not the targets of the insurgency. *You are.* When the mass media show you all the bad things that happen over here, the insurgents cheer. For they know they can never beat us. That's why they fight us the way they do. They are scared as hell, and they should be. This insurgency can never, ever defeat the American military.

But they can beat our hearts. They can cut off our inspiration, and they can do it through your TVs and your newspapers and the Internet. For they know how embedded the media is in our society. They know that if we lose the support of the American public, we lose faith in ourselves. If the mass media had the inclination or the ability to show you all the good work we are doing over here, they would have twenty-four hour continuous coverage, 365 days a year, not American death toll statistics and instances of violence shown between recent Hollywood divorces and the latest headlines. To a news channel, what makes better news, suicide bombers or the reopening of a school in a small village that you will never even think about visiting? And what does the mass media really strive for, compassion or ratings? You decide.

If we, the soldiers and marines and airmen and sailors and men and women of the United States Armed Forces lose your support, then the work we do will truly be in vain. Our inspiration will be dried up, our energy usurped.

If you are too proud to act patriotic and you feel like a hypocrite, then fake it. Do it anyway. Do it for us. Because like I said before, we are you. When you see us on TV, you're looking in the mirror. We are your sons and daughters and moms and dads and friends and neighbors. None of us could have known we would be in an ancient Holy Land in the year 2005, fighting a type of war that has never come before.

So don't cry for us, America; just pray for us. Don't worry—we know how to fight and protect ourselves. Just keep the light on for us, keep the house warm in the winter, wrap the pipes, offer us your support, look after our children, keep yourselves safe as you can until we return, and know that we stare up at the sky often and recall what it's like to be home.

Don't question our reasons for raising a hand and saying, "I do solemnly swear . . ." Just give us the benefit of the doubt. We're doing the best we can, and knowing you're behind us means a lot.

So thank you, American people, for your continued support. Keep the care packages coming, and the brownies cooking. Send those letters. Take those pictures. Have the kids at school make banners. And if you're someone who doesn't know a soldier firsthand, sponsor one. Take care of yourselves, because it's a dangerous world. We worry about you.

We'll be back very soon to savor the American lifestyle once again. And remember—no matter what happens or where they send us, *we* will always support *you*.

Four Years Later—February 6, 2007

Four years later, here we still stand and fight, cycling back to America across the jet stream, across the ocean, to heal, to resupply, and then we return to the desert. Four years and some of us have been here two or three times. We are doing a good job, but it's hard work. Four years and here we lie at night, under these particular constellations, thinking about home. How could we not?

Who is that woman sitting with her knees pulled to her chest in the window on the thirtieth floor of a hotel in New York City staring down at the lights and lost in her own dark thoughts, who, when she focuses her eyes one way can see the scene below her, but when she focuses another way can see her own reflection? What's she thinking about?

And who is that young man in Salt Lake City driving way too fast and tapping his hands on the leather-covered steering wheel as his music thumps, on his way to work, for which he is late again, thinking about his girlfriend and perfectly content because it's payday?

Whose child might that be at the playground, going up the stairs and down the circular slide over and over, smiling at everyone so sweetly and only now gaining enough confidence to try to climb the big red curved ladder?

And who is that girl with the hazel eyes staring intently at a copy of the selected poems of Ralph Waldo Emerson? Isn't she too young to be interested in Emerson? Is she in college? Where does she live? How did she come to be in this library, sitting next to an artificial fireplace for warmth in her lovely beige sweater?

You there, you solitary figure, looking so stoic. I'm in the air outside the window, hovering over the place where the ocean batters the continent. I'm just a drifting thought on a solitary reconnaissance. You're sitting in a lighthouse reading a book by candle. The glow from the flame lights up your bearded cheek. Why read with a candle when you have such a powerful light? Your beam sweeps the land, then casts out over the Atlantic Ocean with a force that is almost natural, as if man did not place it there. It cannot reach the other side. You have no idea how symbolic you are right now, out here on the coast of Maine all alone.

I sense you all out there, though you may think not of me.

And I accept you for what you are, stranger or friend. I need you to be there because you make my homeland what it is. You are all, friends and strangers alike, so sacred in my mind. For what is American life—what is a wait in line at the post office or a drive to the store—without a sea of human faces? Some faces are beautiful, others mean and hateful. Some are inspiring, while others are frightening. But their very presence is part of what makes America great. What are friends if there are no strangers?

The idea of you all begets a powerful memory, a force of nature, an alternate reality, something I would never give up on, a caring voice on the end of a telephone line, a mystery, the smile of an old friend, a nice thought, a funny story, a well-meant gesture.

You dwell out there forming your own self-portrait of America—the trucker driving six hundred miles a day through the snowy mountains of Wyoming, the young boy at football practice in Maryland, the aspiring writer in New York, staring out at the city for inspiration, the jazz singer looking for part-time work in the French Quarter, the grandfather in Arizona who swims two miles a day, the housewife in Pennsylvania who makes scrapbooks for her kids, the young man in Basic Training learning how to become a soldier, the hippie chicks at the University of Montana hanging out on the steps of the Liberal Arts building, the newborn baby in Minnesota lying in her crib and gazing wide-eyed at the shadows created by her night-light, and all the nameless faces and moments that make up our history.

And we love you for it.

> *All wars are civil wars, because all men are brothers.*
> —François Fénelon

IN ORDER TO SEE BEAUTY IN LIFE, I HAD TO SEE HELL

an interview with Staff Sergeant David Bellavia

Staff Sergeant David Bellavia served in Kosovo and then Iraq. As a result of his heroism in the Battle of Fallujah in November 2004, he has been nominated for the Medal of Honor. He wrote about his experiences in House to House. *David is the cofounder of Vets for Freedom.*

Marc Aronson: What led you to enlist?

David Bellavia: I was a theater arts major; I had no interest in joining the army. I loved history, theater, novels: stories that have satisfying endings. But I felt like an empty vessel, with no passion, no drama in my life. I enlisted when we were at peace, so I pictured serving as summer camp with haircuts. My boot camp instructors kept saying that I was getting the kind of training in confidence and leadership that executives pay huge fees to experience—and I was happy to get it. I was stationed in Kosovo, and although there had been terrible civil war there, I felt completely safe—in fact I hardly ever wore my helmet and only menaced someone with a rifle when they would not listen to reason and keep their car moving in traffic.

MA: When did that "summer camp" phase of your enlistment end?

DB: On 9/11, when the two towers in New York fell. I was older, had a family, and had raw eighteen-year-olds, who might never have gone out on dates, looking to me for leadership. I felt an obligation to bring them home, no matter what. I would do anything to fulfill that mission, that responsibility.

MA: Tell me more about what you felt for your men.

DB: No one wants to die. No one says, hey, I want to die at twenty-one. But there is a different feeling: I am willing to put myself at risk of death if my action empowers someone else. If I have a scared kid serving under me, I am going to have to con him; I have to act (in fact I believe the very best background for being a soldier is theater). You must never let anyone know what you feel inside. You have to be this completely stoic, this-is-no-problem, I-am-in-control guy. You give yourself up to lead. In war, if you have a crappy leader, you will lose your life. Once you make that commitment to your men, it allows you to do things that are otherwise completely irrational.

MA: You say that you changed as a result of feeling

that bond, that duty, to your men. How else does combat change soldiers?

DB: If you serve in combat, you will lose your innocence, even your identity. But you are also enriched more than you will ever be back home. I went to basic training with kids who had never seen a black person. They took photos of the black soldiers—they were such an oddity to them. But in battle, they carried each other to safety. I served next to Muslim Americans. We relied on each other, trusted each other.

Life is about service; that is the lesson you find in war. You serve your buddies in combat, or you serve at home. You serve wherever the hell you go. That is what makes life worth living.

MA: Are you in favor of national service where everyone does something after high school?

DB: Absolutely.

MA: Tell me about November 10, 2004.

DB: November 10, 2004, was my birthday. We were in Fallujah, and we had become complacent. Hours had passed without a firefight. And up till then, our fights had been easy—we shoot, we kick in a door, we win. But now we were tired, cold, sick, hungry, and we got fire from a building. The enemy in Fallujah had all kinds of weapons they had captured from us—we were fighting against our best equipment. And they were well trained; we saw them use the very same tactics and techniques we had learned. This was an all-star team of enemy fighters.

Fighting to get control of the building, they began mocking us in English. If a guy was hit and calling for a medic, an enemy soldier would say, "Mommy, Mommy, help me."

I had always dreamed of being a hero—being John Wayne, the one who kicks the door down and clears out the bad guys. I knew this was my moment to live out every tape, every scene I had played out in my head. I panicked. I was so paralyzed I could not move my legs. I thought I must be hurt, shot.

One part of my mind was saying, "Go get 'em," and another said, "What the hell are you talking about? You are a coward, not a hero."

We managed to get out of the building, but they were shooting down at us from the roof. The street was too narrow to bring in support. I could see the faces of my men; they were no longer looking at me to lead them. They knew I just wanted to escape from that building. I had been away for three years, had hardly seen my family. Why? Why had I, had they, sacrificed so much? All of that was for a lie—I did not have the guts to lead. I felt that if I was going to be in Iraq, in the army,

I had better be good. Otherwise it was all a waste, a waste of time, a waste of my life. We would all die here in the street, for nothing.

I felt like it was a battle for my soul: Do you have integrity? Are you a liar? If I could go into that house myself, I would give my guys the power and strength to follow

In order to see beauty in life, I had to see hell, the fucking worst; the only thing that delivered me was rage and hate. In that house fight, I was shooting and killing enemies all around me. But there was one guy I grabbed, tried to subdue. I had him in a choke hold; he bit my arm. I started to beat and beat him; I pulled a knife and slashed his throat while I held him. I was not a person anymore; I was an animal. I thought of nothing but myself, my survival. I was a freaking dog, an animal.

And then, after, when I came down from that hate and rage, I had such an empty and worthless feeling.

To this day, I don't want to be in a fight, even an argument, again. Because I don't know what could happen. I learned how animalistic I could become. I live my life never to be near that place again, never to get back into it. That is the cross you have to bear. The more people experience combat, the more people there are who will never go to war again.

MA: You describe the battle as this shaping moment, the very worst human experience, but in some way also calling for your very best. If you were standing in a high school and a group of students was thinking about enlisting and asked you what to do, what would you say?

DB: I'd say, "Do it." I have two boys, and I absolutely hope they serve. Maybe not in the infantry, but somewhere. The military shows you middle America—the ignorant, the brilliant, the religious, the whores, the drug addicts—everyone, and you learn to get along. And what chance does an eighteen-year-old have to see the world?

But you need to be realistic. If you join the army, it is for eight years, and you will be deployed. We are fighting now, and will be fighting in the future. Before you sign up, read Philip Caputo's *A Rumor of War;* read Stephen Ambrose's *Citizen Soldiers;* read my book—I am the worst character in my own book; in combat I became a hollow, empty, soulless person. You need to know that before you join. War is not glamorous; it is not glorious. And we as a nation cannot fight on the cheap—we should fight when we all agree to it, when we all serve, when we are committed to win, and when we have an exit strategy, a way to leave with honor. But all that said, when you are needed, you have to go.

MA: In his piece for this book, C. W. Bowman Jr. talks about the shattering experience of returning to Vietnam years later and realizing the enemy were human, just like him. Is that the same in Iraq?

DB: No. One big difference between us and previous generations of soldiers is that in an all-volunteer army, with the media coverage, we know the enemy is human. We know we cannot just bomb a house, a village, an enemy-controlled area—the film will be all over the world and make us more enemies. But that also means you keep holding back, restraining, seeing your buddies get hit, resting your feet on a body bag holding your pal in it. And then when you get into a fight, and it is a real fight, those months of waiting come pouring out. In a way, it is worse, because we have to keep holding back under fire.

The Persian Gulf War made everyone think it would be easy—*Star Wars,* just a few casualties. When America sends its young people to fight, it has to be realistic about what they will face.

TOUGH

by Joel Turnipseed

Joel Turnipseed served in the Marine Corps during the Persian Gulf War. He went on to write an article about his experiences in GQ magazine, which he expanded into the memoir Baghdad Express. *He has received many grants and fellowships, including a Minnesota State Arts Board fellowship. He continues to write and teach in Minnesota.*

We laughed at "tough." We had all been to the world's greatest school in tough: Marine Corps boot camp. We knew too much about the various ways of tough: hard-asses getting their butts kicked in bar fights outside Jacksonville, North Carolina; other guys who could take anything; the worst life had to offer. Took it like it was ladled into a canteen cup just for them. We had seen the sad, hard coldness and resignation of the tough guy. Nonetheless, tough was one of those Marine Corps traditions too hard to shake, like booze and women and tattoos. Which meant that when we laughed at "tough," we were laughing at ourselves. When we went to war, we added wicked new moves to this dance—acting especially tough and becoming even more savage in our mockery.

Our war started in August 1990, as we were activated as marine reservists and sent to the four winds: Twentynine Palms and Camp Pendleton in California, Cherry Point and Camp Lejeune in North Carolina. Then, in January of 1991, we reassembled in Saudi Arabia for war with Saddam Hussein. It didn't turn out to be much of a war—unless you were one of the tens of thousands of dead Iraqis at the end, but it started out with some pretty good fireworks. Saddam at least put on a *show* of fighting the Mother of All Battles. He entertained us with four or five Scud attacks the first night of the war, but the end result was just another morning formation in the Corps.

The smoking lamp was lit, and we were standing by to stand by. The worst injury any of us had gotten in those first attacks was an M-16 jammed up our ass during a blind jump into a bunker. But life and war have their smaller ways of showing the pointlessness of "tough"—"It's the little shit that kills you," screamed our drill instructors. For all its fighting fame, the Marine Corps' traditions also include such soul-killing tediousness as spending whole days raking dirt or painting rocks or picking up cigarette butts from acres of dead grass. No one knows how to turn a perfectly placid morning into an honest-to-goodness bitch like a Marine Corps staff sergeant or gunnery sergeant. When we finally got around to attention, our company gunny informed us that we suffered a severe shortage of sandbags, had nowhere near enough bunkers, that we expected more Scud attacks tonight and every other night, that Saddam Hussein wasn't going to go quietly, that he wanted to fuck us up, that we were down range, and so: "You gentlemen are going to take a little field trip out to the *real* Bumfuck Egypt. You've got ten minutes to square away your trash and get on the trucks. You'll need your weapons, extra water— and your E-tools."

"E-tool." Sounds like very high-tech, sexy Marine Corps munitions, I know—but this meant that we'd be building bunker parts with a two-foot foldable shovel: the entrenching tool. And so half our company piled onto truck beds crammed with pallets of empty plastic sandbags.

"Who's the smart-ass," asked Bergmann, "who sent these things over here *empty*? I mean, *really,* isn't this one of the things they could have fucked up, too?"

Like I said, it's the little things.

We grabbed our gear and climbed onto the truck: packs with E-tools dangling from them and stuffed with chemical weapons suits and rat-fucked food items: extra Tabasco, peanut butter and crackers, coffee packets, and ass-wipes. We also carried our rifles, body armor, and a couple ammo boxes of Sterno tabs Heinemann managed to scrounge up on a supply tent recon mission.

Did we look tough, bumping down the road in the back of the five-ton? Hell if we knew— most of us didn't *care*—but a few guys tried to look the part. When we were stopped over in Torrejón, Spain, waiting for our final jump to Saudi, we saw some guys wearing knives on their shins: bottom grommet laced to their boot and the top of the sheath strapped just below their knees with a cutoff canvas belt. Rocky, Joseph, Heinemann, Blegen, and a few other guys imitated this getup, walking with a kind of swagger. I don't know—how bad-assed do you need to look when you're sandbagging? But there they were: M-16s between their knees as we bounced out into the desert, with Ka-Bar fighting knives on their shins.

We drove out a few miles into the desert and began digging. By the time we had filled the first few hundred bags, we were standing in holes four or five feet deep. Just deep enough so that we were gazing at ground level as a column of army M1 Abrams tanks arrived at our perimeter. They must have gotten a pretty good laugh out of our sorry asses: with our mismatched green helmets and brown chocolate-chip desert uniforms, we didn't look so much like marines as dancing bushes popping out of gopher holes. *They,* on the other hand, looked like *the shit*. Maybe they even looked tough. As they got out of their tanks, they pulled their goggles back and their bandanas down and let loose. One dude, in particular, struck a particularly bad pose: resting his M-16 with M-203 grenade-launcher attachment against his hip, he lit up a smoke and stood on the deck of the tank, a long slow cloud of cool trailing past him.

"Jesus Christ on a Popsicle stick," said Bergmann with a laugh, "would you look at *that* asshole? Who the fuck does he think he is, Lawrence of Arabia?"

"No," said Boogard, "more like the Marlboro Man."

"I don't know," cried Rocky. "I think he looks *awesome*! I can't wait to get that salty."

It's in a day's work for marines to get grabasstic: a work party seldom ends without a monkey pile and you receiving a hard elbow to the ear as you're trying to give some other poor bastard lower down in the scrum a knee to the kidney. Rocky's wistful glare at the Marlboro Man brought a hysterical bout of laughter all around. Followed by his swift upending.

"You want to be salty, Rocky?" asked Heinemann.

Still not getting it, Rocky made the mistake of answering, "Fuckin' A!"

A quick look between Heinemann and Boogard resulted in Rocky upside down with his head in the sand and his boots twisting in the sky.

For starters, they gave Rocky a sand-hole swirly, then lifted him up for air just long enough for him to scream—a cry of "Fuck y—" stifled by a second trip into the sand, filling his mouth with true grit.

"Hey, Rocky," cried Joseph, "you're *starting* to look salty."

"What do you think? Is he salty enough yet?" asked Boogard as he yanked Rocky up by the back of his pants and Heinemann clutched his beet-red face in a full nelson.

"No!!!!"

Were we a little hard on Rocky? Tough, maybe? Maybe. But what's tough, anyway? When I was thirteen, I watched my father nail his hand to a stair with a nail gun. It was a pretty impressive sight, but more impressive was watching him mutter, low and smooth, with a cigarette in one corner of his mouth, "Gimme a hammer, wouldya?" And so I handed him a hammer and watched him claw his hand up from the raw pine board of the staircase he was building. And then pound the nail out the other side, and, cigarette still dangling from his lips, yell, "Get me some duct tape!" And then we went back to work. Whenever I tell this story, I laugh and people look at me like I'm completely insane.

It wasn't *my* hand, of course, but it was an object lesson I took to heart when getting my ribs caved in underneath the public schools stadium, or my helmet turned 180 degrees when trying to tackle a running back who outweighed me by a hundred pounds. You dust yourself off and hold back the hurt. And laugh—and then you go off and join the Marine Corps. And laugh some more, laugh even harder, at even more incredibly stupid and painful shit.

"Is the Marine Corps tough?" If you made it through August two-a-days in football practice or ever made weight for wrestling in February, you're not going to have a problem with the Corps. If you have average intelligence and have suffered at least one or two hard knocks in life, the Marine Corps designed its boot camp just for *you*. Isn't that great? Just for you. After playground bullying, drunk fathers, and locker-room high jinks, the mind-fucking of the drill instructors and the petty sadism of a really bad NCO in the fleet are just another day at work. Hell, they even teach you how to *gripe* in boot camp. Sing along with me: "Hey, ho, diddly-bop-bop, I wish I was back on the block-block. Oh, with a bottle in my hand—I want to be a drinkin' man."

No, it's not tough that's an issue most of the time, but bullshit. Tough is a joke, but bullshit will positively suck the life out of you. And Rocky invoked bullshit's holy name right about the time that Heinemann had him yanked up by the back of his pants and Boogaard was stuffing sand in his skivvies.

"Thipth ditz *bullspthit!*"

"Sound off like you got a pair, Rocky! We can't *hear you!*" yelled Heinemann.

And then he spoke up: he had managed to pull his Ka-Bar from its sheath and cut Boogard's arm from elbow to wrist. That's the old actions-speak-louder-than-words at work! It wasn't very tough, though. Very bullshit, we thought—really, absolutely a bullshit move.

"Holy fuck!" screamed Boogard, tossing Rocky down into one of the sand pits.

"Now *that's* salty!" cried Bergmann. "Jesus Christ, Rocky—are you *insane*?"

The blood was spurting from the vein in Boogard's arm as he ripped his T-shirt from his chest to use it as a compression bandage. While he struggled to get the bleeding under control, his hands sloppy with blood and sand, we laughed.

After a while we all stopped together and looked at each other, as if to say, "Are we really this fucking stupid?" A brief moment of silence answered, "Yes."

Boogard went for a ride to get stitches. He told the corpsman that he cut himself playing around with a Ka-Bar. Rocky got endless shit for the rest of the war. Bergmann continued to be a totally hilarious pain in the ass. Blegen left the Marine Corps under questionable circumstances. Joseph was killed in a rollover. That was tough *and* bullshit: and that was blind bad luck, and sad. Joseph's A-driver became a kind of ghost in our tents: he didn't talk after watching his best friend get killed—not the rest of the war. He had messed up his back and neck, but those weren't the wounds he carried out of the Corps. We heard rumors for years afterward about his decline: coke habit, drinking, pissing away his disability pay . . . And for some reason we laughed at that, too, when we traded the rumors out in the field.

Most of us got through the Marine Corps and the war OK. A few of us even became successful adult human beings. But whatever premonitions we had of our individual fates, during that morning and the other early days of the war—before exhaustion and rumor and death just sort of took over—none of it mattered at that moment: because we were laughing at "tough," at wanting to be a hard-ass, at wanting to be at war. Because it *was* funny—just like it was funny when my dad asked me for that hammer or when M from Platoon 3068 fell forty feet from the rappel tower in boot camp because he was afraid to go down on a rope he tied around his waist or when B tried to kill himself by shaving off his wrist with a Bic single-blade safety razor. We had already learned too much about "tough" to take it seriously—even if it's hardest lessons were still to come.

To laugh at these things, it's true, requires a little damage beforehand—that a certain part of you has been damaged—*fucked,* actually—but once you've arrived at that crooked branch on the human tree, it becomes *necessary* to laugh at these things: impossible not to. Completely, unbelievably fucked-up shit happens every day in the Marine Corps. And you will learn to laugh at it. Hard laughs. And someday afterward, when you laugh at the wrong thing, at the wrong time, in the wrong company, and feel like hell for it, you will realize that "tough" is like a little gremlin, one that has been waiting and watching—Always Faithful—just sort of goofing around off to the side of your life, waiting to get the *last* laugh back at you. And he will.

A SURVIVOR'S TALE

a Nagasaki memoir by Fumiko Miura

The nuclear bomb dropped by America on Nagasaki in 1945 ended World War II as far as our hostilities with Japan were concerned and ushered in the Atomic Age, changing the face of war forever. In the following selection, distinguished Japanese poet Fumiko Miura, who was then a sixteen-year-old resident of the city, remembers that apocalyptic day. Notice that the citizens of Nagasaki had not been told that the first nuclear bomb had been dropped on Hiroshima just three days earlier.

Fumiko Miura is professor emeritus at Keio University, Tokyo. She is the author of a collection of tanka poems, Pinku no Kobara, *and* Pages from the Seasons, *translated by James Kirkup, which includes both tanka poems quoted below.*

August ninth approaches, and I am reminded again of the atomic bombing of Nagasaki fifty-seven years ago, when I was a sixteen-year-old schoolgirl. I'm seventy-three now, and even now I seem to hear screams for help. That one plutonium bomb killed 74,000 people and heavily injured 75,000. It had the explosive power of 21,000 tons of TNT, and the temperature of the ground at the hypocenter of the explosion rose in a flash to 3,000 to 4,000 degrees. Almost everyone within four kilometers [two and a half miles] of the explosion was burned and killed, or received external injuries.

The 240,000 citizens of Nagasaki were quite unprepared for the attack. I remember the air-raid warning sounded early that morning, but a few hours later it was cancelled—I don't remember exactly when, but probably before eight o'clock. It was a scorchingly hot day; from daybreak, cicadas were singing loudly. In the air-raid shelter, we were sweating profusely in our padded hoods and long-sleeved jackets, which were supposed to protect us against burns and injuries.

So it was a relief when the warning was cancelled, and we removed our padded hoods and returned to our duties. Following a government order issued in February 1944, middle- and high-school students throughout Japan were recruited to work at weapons manufacturing plants or at places related to the military. The Japanese people, regardless of age and sex, worked, offering their precious lives in "a heroic sacrifice" to carry out the *seisen,* or sacred war. We were taught to become faithful *shiko no mitate*—humble shields for the Emperor.

I was doing some clerical work for the Japanese Imperial Army. At about eleven o'clock, I thought I heard the throb of a B-29 circling over the two-story army headquarters building. I wondered why an American bomber was flying around above us when we had been given the all-clear. There was no noise of anti-aircraft fire. We were working in our shirtsleeves, and all the windows and doors were wide open because it was so stiflingly hot and humid in our two-story building.

At that moment, a horrible flash, thousands of times as powerful as lightning, hit me. I felt that it almost rooted out my eyes. Thinking that a huge bomb had exploded above our building, I jumped up from my seat and was hit by a tremendous wind, which smashed down windows, doors, ceilings, and walls, and shook the whole building. I remember trying to run for the stairs before being knocked to the floor and losing consciousness. It was a hot blast, carrying splinters of glass and concrete debris. But it did not have that burning heat of the hypocenter, where everyone and everything was melted in an instant by the heat flash. I learned later that the heat decreased with distance. I was 2,800 meters [1¾ miles] away from the hypocenter.

When I came to, it was evening. I was lying in the front yard of the headquarters—I still do not know how I got there—covered with countless splinters of glass, wood, and concrete, and losing blood from both arms. I felt dull pains all over my body. My white short-sleeved blouse and *mompe* (the authorities had ordered women, young and old, to wear these Japanese-style loose trousers) were torn and bloody. I felt strangely calm. I looked down at my wristwatch; it was completely broken.

I sat in a field of rubble watching the sun set. I thought this was the end of Nagasaki, and of Japan. I prayed that my family might have escaped injuries and be alive. I had been taught to believe that the *kamikaze* (divine wind) would blow someday to save Japan from crisis, leading us to a decisive victory, but realized that there was no divine wind to attack the American plane; instead, a bomb of huge power had exploded over us, when we were totally unprepared.

Blessed by fate, I was allowed to survive. But my normal wartime routine had suddenly been interrupted by death and horror. I felt guilty for being alive. I learned later that the primary target for this second bomb had been Kokura, the largest industrial city in northern Kyushu; Nagasaki, which was a shipbuilding center, was the secondary target. On that morning of August ninth, when the bomber named *Bockscar* reached the sky over Kokura, clouds hung heavily over the city, and the plane, now running low on fuel, turned toward Nagasaki. When it reached the center of Nagasaki city, visibility was still poor. So it moved 3,300 meters [about two miles] northwest and found a hole in the cloud large enough to drop a bomb through. It exploded at 11:02.

Many people were trapped under fallen debris; some who survived the blast were burned to death when subsequent fires raged through the city. Charred bodies lay scattered on the red wasteland. I wrote some poems about the inhuman attack:

> Blown out by the bomb
> a horse's intestines are
> scattered all around;
> a half-immolated cat,
> crazed with hunger, attacks them.

> A half-naked woman
> her throat and mouth blasted by
> the heat rays, holding
> a baby that keeps seeking
> milk from her mother's breast.

With no detailed information about the "new type of bomb" issued by the government, we did not know for about a week that it was actually the atomic bomb. We learned that the Soviet Union had declared war on Japan on the day of the Nagasaki atomic bombing. I was infuriated at our government, which still urged us to fight against the Allied Forces. We were injured, and suffering from a strange weakness with no adequate treatment. Food, clothes, information: eveything was in shortage. Yet the government still shouted its slogan: *"Ichioku gyokusai!"* ("One hundred million people should meet honorable deaths! Never surrender!") Who did the Japanese government exist for? I wondered.

Shortly after the explosion, many survivors noticed in themselves a strange illness: vomiting; loss of appetite; diarrhea; high fever; weakness; purple spots on various parts of the body; bleeding from the mouth, gums, and throat; the falling out of hair, and a very low white blood cell count. We called the illness "atomic bomb disease," and many of those who were only superficially injured died soon or months after. The lack of medical supplies and information about the aftereffects of atomic radiation made it impossible to provide us with adequate treatment. First aid was all we could get.

Decades afterward, I had a series of operations for cancer, which may be attributable to my having been exposed to radiation. However, I am not yet destroyed. With the blessing of gods and Buddha, I have been allowed to live. For the sake of those who were killed without mercy during and after the Nagasaki atomic bombing, and also for myself, I want to be able to survive for many more years. My physical being may be transient, but I believe that my spiritual being can remain undefeated. I wish sincerely that human beings will become wise enough to abandon all forms of nuclear weapons in the near future.

THE
AFTERMATH
OF WAR

KILLING FLIES

a one-act play by Rita Williams-Garcia

Rita Williams-Garcia's six novels for teenagers have earned her the reputation as a popular author for young adults. Novels such as Like Sisters on the Homefront, Every Time a Rainbow Dies, *and* Fast Talk on a Slow Track *have been honored by PEN; the Bologna Book Fair; the Coretta Scott King committee; every major review publication; and states including New York, New Jersey, Kentucky, Tennessee, and Texas. As the daughter of a career army officer, she saw the country while her family moved to different army bases from coast to coast.*

"For as long as my family has been in this country, someone has been wearing a military uniform and fighting a war," she says. "I brought my father to school for show-and-tell in the second and sixth grade. The first time was after he graduated from Officer Candidate School, and the last was when he returned from Vietnam. I didn't set out to marry a military man, but Sergeant Peter Garcia and I found we had much in common. His mother was a WAC in the all-black 6888th Battalion during World War II and my sister is an air force veteran. I remember holding my children while Peter marched with his unit for deployment to Desert Storm. To this day, fife and drums make me tear. I know someone is going off to war."

CAST
PFC Ada Green, 20, Iraq War vet
Big Ma, 70, Ada's grandmother
Raquel, 30, Ada's sister
Nell, 10, Ada's niece
Wit Bit, 5, Ada's nephew
Specialist Bonner, female soldier, voice-over only
Sergeant Sanchez, Ada's NCO, voice-over only

Scene 1
5:00 A.M. Front view of a row house with a screened-in porch in Germantown, Philadelphia. An American flag hangs limp in the front yard on a stale summer night. Vestiges of a welcome-home celebration from two days earlier are evident from yellow ribbons littering the front yard and a WELCOME HOME, ADA banner trailing out of a garbage can.

  The main action takes place on the porch, screened in like an extra-large chicken coop. There are two doors, one leading to the front entrance of the Green house, the other out into the yard. In the center of the porch is a flat cot minus pillow or bedding and on top, PFC ADA GREEN lies on her back in a guarded sleep. She is desert-tanned, muscular, still wearing sand-colored camouflage pants, an army-issue T-shirt, and beige socks. Her Ranger hat is slid down over her face. At the foot of her cot stands a body-size duffel bag. At the head of the duffel bag sits her Kevlar helmet with dark sun goggles still strapped to it as though they're watching her. A pair of desert boots stands ready at the base of the duffel bag.

PFC Green shifts in her sleep, mumbling, although nothing intelligible can be made out. One minute she is peaceful, the next minute restless. Ada alternates between answering Sergeant Sanchez, her NCO, and Specialist Bonner, another female soldier in her unit. Although the audience can't see them, both audience and Ada hear Sanchez's and Bonner's voices, as if they are coming from the duffel bag.

A lone porch light illuminates the otherwise nearly dark scene.

BONNER: I think they stopped.

GREEN: They're reloading. Stay down.

BONNER: It's quiet. They stopped.

GREEN: Just stay down. Be ready. Be ready. Be ready. . . .

> (There is a SUDDEN THUNK against the
> front screen. In one smooth motion, Ada
> rolls out of the cot into a crouching position.
> Ada is sleepwalking, but looks to the duffel

bag, holds her hand out, motioning Bonner
to stay low. She scans the outer perimeter
and sees there is no one. The audience sees
it's only a newspaper.)

GREEN *(to duffel bag)*: All clear.

(Ada rises slowly, rolls back onto the cot, and
slides her Ranger hat down over her eyes.)

(A half hour passes. It's still fairly dark
as dawn approaches. BIG MA opens front
door. She sees Ada still sleeping out on
the porch, shakes her head, and enters
the porch.)

BIG MA: Ada, baby. You still camped out here?

(Ada rolls over and pulls up her Ranger hat
to reveal her face.)

ADA: Yeah, Ma.

BIG MA: When you coming in?

ADA: Little while.

BIG MA: You said that yesterday. *(Beat.)* And the
day before.

ADA: I came in.

BIG MA: When?

ADA: Couple times.

BIG MA: Couple trips to the downstairs toilet
don't count.

ADA: Sure they do. You don't want me unloading
on the porch.

BIG MA: Ada Jane Green! What am I gonna do
with you?

ADA: Just let me sleep awhile. I can't get to sleep.
Can't get peaceful.

BIG MA: Aren't you dying of thirst? You can't be
out here without no water. All this heat.

ADA: Can't drink at night. Can't do that. You
drink. Gotta go. Not safe.

BIG MA *(long pause)*: You know you're home,
right.

ADA: 'Course I do. I know I'm here. I know I'm
home. Back in the world.

BIG MA: Then act like you know it. Come on inside. Wash that war off ya. Go on up to your room
and pick out something fresh and girly. Like you
used to back in high school.

ADA *(laughs)*: High school.

(Big Ma opens screen door, bends down with
effort, and picks up the newspaper. She
takes one look at the front page, shakes her
head, and steps back inside the porch.)

ADA: Big Ma.

BIG MA: What is it, baby?

ADA *(sits up)*: Something I been meaning to say.
Been wanting to say in person. Face to face.

BIG MA *(looking over paper)*: What's on your
mind?

ADA: Thanks, Big Ma. That's what I wanted to
say. Thanks.

(Big Ma is puzzled. She lowers the
newspaper.)

ADA: For the letters. The peppermint candies.

BIG MA *(dismissive)*: Prayed more'n I wrote.

ADA: Then you prayed plenty.

BIG MA: You here, aren't you? *(Beat, as ADA nods.)* Well all right, then.

ADA *(not specifically to Big Ma)*: Loved getting letters at mail call. Real paper in my hands. Needed those. And the peppermints.

BIG MA: Butterscotch, too.

ADA: It takes sixteen minutes to suck a peppermint. Sixteen if I don't bite down. That's how I count time. We go out on a mission. Go hand out supplies. Raid a house—all the same thing. A mission. I pop a peppermint and count time. Be sharp, be ready, sixteen minutes at a time.

BIG MA: Well, you're home, Ada Jane. Can have all the peppermints you want.

(Big Ma puts her arms around Ada, which gives Ada a small startle. Ada recovers quickly.)

(Big Ma wrinkles her nose, draws back, and fans herself with the newspaper.)

BIG MA (*firm*): Today, Ada Jane. You're getting in that tub today.

ADA: I will. I will. Just tired. But I can't sleep. Can't get (*trails off*) peaceful . . .

(Big Ma exits inside house.)

Scene 2

A half hour passes. Dark gives way to a smoky, pale blue. Ada sleeps in a reclined position with her Ranger hat pulled down over her face, ready to get up at a moment's notice.

SANCHEZ: Here she comes. Slow-moving vehicle.

GREEN: Looks like a woman driver, Sarge.

SANCHEZ: Stand ready, Green.

GREEN: Ready, Sarge.

(TWO LOUD CAR HONKS from the street.)

GREEN: Car bomb!

(Ada reaches down inside her sock for a sidearm. She comes up with her hand pointed in the direction of the street, as if her hand were a gun. She's calm. Ready.)

(The HORN BLOWS again. RAQUEL enters from the house into the porch. Raquel, a harried single mother, wears nurse's scrubs and totes a huge shoulder bag.)

RAQUEL: Out here again, brat? What's wrong? Too hot inside?

(Ada comes out of it, realizing she's at home in Germantown.)

ADA: I like it out here. Cooler.

RAQUEL: Start liking it inside. *(Gets a whiff of Ada and swats the air.)* Girl!

ADA: Yeah, yeah.

RAQUEL: You need a good soak. *(Beat.)* You're not still using those wet naps I sent ya. You're home, brat. We have a tub, a shower, a sink, soap, and hot water inside the house, up those stairs.

ADA: Yeah, thanks for sending those, sis. The wet naps. You don't know . . .

RAQUEL: Wasn't nothing.

ADA: You don't know . . .

RAQUEL: Well, look. Here's what I know. I'm late for work. I need you to take Wit Bit to the park till noon.

(Ada turns over.)

RAQUEL: Big Ma can't be out in all this heat running after Wit Bit. Your days of adventurama and seeing the whole wide world are over, brat. You're home. Be useful. Take Wit Bit to the park.

ADA: We'll see.

(HORN BLOWS.)

RAQUEL *(yells to car, stage right)*: JUST A MINUTE! *(Fishes a five-dollar bill from her bag.)* Get him an Italian ice. Push him on the swing. A couple of ups and downs on the seesaw. Just take a shower, Ada! You're killing flies out here.

(Raquel is not convinced Ada hears her. She HITS the cot—*bang, bang, bang*. Ada reaches around and swiftly grabs Raquel's wrist. Ada could probably kill in her sleep if necessary.)

RAQUEL *(struggling)*: Let go, brat. My ride is waiting.

ADA: Let me sleep. I can't sleep.

(Raquel wrenches her arm free and rubs her wrist.)

RAQUEL: Been asleep for two days while some of us are out here working.

(HORN BLOWS again. Raquel exits out front screen door.)

RAQUEL *(offstage)*: Take a shower and take Wit Bit to the park!

(Ada falls back into a restless sleep. A few minutes pass.)

BONNER: Walk me to the latrine.

GREEN: Told you not to drink all that water.

BONNER: Come with me, Green. Can't go by myself. You know what happens when we go alone.

GREEN: I know.

BONNER: Damned men. A girl can't drop her pants and pee. Just think they can—

GREEN: Don't worry, Bonner. I got you covered. Got you covered. Got you covered. . . .

Scene 3
A half hour passes. Now early daylight, the porch light goes out. It's not a scorcher yet, but it will be.

NELL enters the porch from the house carrying a backpack. Her school wear suggests that she's eager for her teen years to begin.

NELL *(waves arms against the odor)*: Hooo gravy!

   (Ada hears Nell but doesn't react.)

NELL: Auntie, I love you. Glad you're home, but you stink. No offense.

ADA: Don't make me hug you.

NELL: Better not, bad as you smell!

ADA *(turns over and holds out her arms)*: Give Auntie love. Big love.

NELL: I'm giving Auntie soap. Big soap and

water. Hoo gravy! I'm gonna do you like you used to do me back in the day.

ADA: What you know about back in the day?

NELL: I'm gonna chase you round the sofa, grab you by the foot, drag you to the tub, and throw you in the hot soapy drink.

ADA: See me running?

NELL *(exasperated)*: Come on, Auntie. My friends'll be here any minute.

ADA: So. Let 'em come.

NELL *(stamps feet)*: Not with you out on the porch smelling up the place. All this stuff out here like we're in a war zone. Just go inside, Auntie. I'll bring those army things in the house—

(Nell takes a step toward the duffel bag. Ada springs up and blocks Nell from it.)

ADA *(sharp)*: Don't touch that.

NELL: Dag, Auntie.

ADA: I mean it. Don't touch that.

NELL (*backing down*): OK, OK. You're so jumpy. (*Beat.*) You should let me run you a bath. Squeeze in a drop of cherry blossom body wash from the mall. That's exactly what you need, Auntie.

ADA: I just need a little air. That's all. A little air. A little longer.

NELL: Ooh! Let me pick you out something nice to wear.

(Nell points to Ada's army fatigues.)

Get you outta (with contempt) *those*. You have nice clothes in your closet, Auntie. Skirts. Tops. Heels. Not that I tried them on while you're gone. I'm just saying. Nice stuff.

ADA: Ooh. That was a nice breeze.

NELL (*waving hands*): Auntie. My friends'll be here. Soon.

ADA: So?

NELL: Please, Auntie. Please, please, please get up.

ADA: In a minute.

NELL: I'm telling Big Ma you out here stinking. *(Looks down near the cot.)* Are those dead flies?

ADA (not hearing Nell): You know I'm right in between you? Right in the middle.

NELL: What?

ADA: You, me, your mother. Ten, twenty, thirty.

NELL: So?

ADA: Used to bathe you, dress you, knot your hair, push you round the park in your stroller.

NELL (heaves a sigh): Once upon a time, back in the day, when I couldn't walk or talk.

ADA: You're talking plenty now.

NELL: And walking.

(Nell does a dance.)

ADA: But not writing.

NELL (stops dancing): I wrote.

ADA: If you want to call three letters in twelve months writing.

The Aftermath of War

NELL: Auntie, you said no e-mail.

ADA: And I meant it.

NELL: Everyone sends e-mail. Everyone.
Dee Dee Trotter's brother's over there. She sends
e-mail and he sends back pictures. Pictures of
him with his AK, leaning on his Humvee with
his crew.

ADA: Unit.

NELL: Crew. Unit. What's the difference?

ADA: Army, unit. Navy, crew. I'm army.

NELL: Got that right. You wear it, won't even get
rid of it, and my friends'll be here. Soon.

ADA: A letter you write at a desk with grooves
dug in from wasting time drawing hearts when
you're supposed to be studying. A letter you lick
closed with Crush soda or Yoo-hoo chocolate still
on your lips. A letter you drop in the mailbox on
Broad Street or at the post office on Union. A
letter you get in your hands and tear it open and
know someone you pushed in the stroller and
knotted their hair and chased until you grabbed
their foot from under the bed thought about you.
A letter you get in your hands from home.

(OFFSTAGE VOICES call out:
NELL-LAAAY!! NELL-LAAAY!!)

NELL: Gotta go!

(Nell kisses her aunt on the forehead and
runs out through the front screen door.)

Scene 4

Early morning, bright sun. Ada tosses and turns,
Ranger hat over her face, still determined to sleep.

SANCHEZ: Don't get too comfy, Green.

GREEN: No, Sarge.

SANCHEZ: Hear me, Green? Don't get too comfortable at home, hanging out at the mall, buying
lip gloss and that thong underwear.

GREEN: No, Sarge.

SANCHEZ: Wake up and find your ass redeployed in a heartbeat.

GREEN: In a heartbeat, Sarge.

SANCHEZ: Damned right, Green. Stand ready
for your orders.

GREEN: Yes, Sarge.

(The screen door opens. Wearing pajama bottoms, Wit Bit enters the porch area. He climbs up in the cot with Ada.)

WIT BIT: Auntie. Auntie.

ADA: What you want, Wit Bit.

WIT BIT: Big Ma say she got coffee.

ADA: OK.

WIT BIT (*shakes Ada*): Auntie.

ADA: What?

WIT BIT: Big Ma say give me a bath.

ADA: In a minute.

WIT BIT: Auntie.

ADA: What?

WIT BIT: Who's that man?

(Ada looks up to see the man.)

WIT BIT *(points to duffel bag)*: That man.

ADA: Don't worry about him.

WIT BIT: I hear y'all talking.

ADA *(embarrassed laugh)*: You do? Must be dreaming out loud.

WIT BIT: I dream out loud. When it's a bad dream. The monster be chasing me and I say, "No, no, no!" And Nell say, "Hush up, Wit Bit."

ADA: Hush up, Wit Bit.

WIT BIT: Hush up, Auntie. *(Long pause.)* Auntie. You like my pictures?

ADA: Yeah, Wit Bit. I like your pictures.

WIT BIT: Which one?

ADA: You sent a million.

WIT BIT: But which one?

ADA: The dog.

WIT BIT: That wasn't no dog. That was a rabbit.

ADA: Was not.

WIT BIT *(beat)*: You going back soon, Auntie?

ADA: Why you ask me that?

WIT BIT *(points)*: *He* wants you to go back.

ADA: I know.

WIT BIT: Don't go, Auntie.

ADA: I gotta go.

WIT BIT: He can't make you.

ADA: No, Wit Bit. He can't make me.

WIT BIT: Then don't go.

ADA: I gotta go. I'm a soldier. Gotta be ready for my orders.

WIT BIT: Don't go, Auntie. Play robots with me.

ADA: I'm tired, Wit Bit. I'm so tired.

WIT BIT: Auntie. You gonna take me to the park?

ADA *(screams into her Ranger hat)*:
AAAARRGGGH!

(Wit Bit isn't bothered by his aunt's
frustration.)

WIT BIT: But Big Ma say I can't go until I have
my bath. You gon' do me like you used to do Nell?

ADA: What?

WIT BIT: Chase me and catch me and throw me
in the tub?

ADA: I guess.

(Wit Bit screams with excitement. He jumps
up and runs into the house. Ada still lies on
the cot, in one last-ditch effort to sleep. The
door opens. Wit Bit sticks his head out.)

WIT BIT: Chase me, Auntie. You 'posed to chase
me.

ADA *(into Ranger hat)*: AAAARRGGHH!

(Ada puts one heavy foot on the ground.
Then the other. Wit Bit screams with de-
light, runs inside and upstairs.)

(Ada slowly pushes herself up and off the cot. She yawns, stretches, and crosses over to door leading into the house. She opens the front door and enters, one heavy foot after the other.)

WAR IS . . .

HEADS

a story by Margo Lanagan

Australian writer Margo Lanagan has published three volumes of stunning short stories in the U.S.: Black Juice *(a Michael L. Printz Honor Book),* White Time, *and* Red Spikes. *In this haunting fantasy tale, we see the aftermath of war in an imaginary great city that has recently been ruined. In the ensuing amoral chaos, a young survivor finds a symbol of the ordered life he has lost and uses it to search for a way to regain meaning.*

Sheegeh pulled a flimsy thing out of the heap.

"Ah, one of these," he said.

Doppo looked up. "Can you eat it?" That was always his first question, so they didn't get loaded down with useless stuff. "It's too little to burn. Could use it as a starter, maybe."

"No, it's special, this one." Sheegeh cleaned the dirt-clots off the strip of paper with its printed numbers. "It's all there, see? The whole thing. Not even torn."

Holding the strip was like lifting a very small, brightly lit box to his eye. His mother was in that box in her pale-blue hospital uniform. She looked tired. She reached her hand into her pocket for something—her handkerchief, maybe, or a list she had written herself, of things to do—but a paper tape like the one Sheegeh was holding came out instead, rolled up neatly. She was a great roller and folder and tucker-away of things. She put this on the table distractedly. Father was calling news from another room beyond this box. (And there were farther rooms, two for sleeping, one for bathing and toileting, and a hallway, and cupboards all over the place that were as good as rooms in themselves; any one of those cupboards would be an excellent home, these days. It wasn't like the Duwazza house, which was like a cage full of mice piled all on top of one another.) *What is that?* said the little invisible Sheegeh at the table, reaching for the rolled thing.

"It's for measuring the babies' heads," he said to Doppo now. "At the hospital, when they're born." There being no babies handy, he put it around his own head and held it flat with a fingertip between his eyes. "What's mine?"

Doppo looked blankly at the finger, then screwed up his forehead to say that Sheegeh was mad. "How useful is that?"

Sheegeh didn't know. Useful? Useful? The little box was so full of colors—the bright calendar picture, the red doors of the cupboards, that pearly-green table. Everything in the box had been brushed and rubbed with cloths and cleansing powders, or soaked with waters and dried crisp in sunlight and clean air. Mother was trying to make dinner in her head and listen to Father and talk with Sheegeh and remember what she'd dipped her hand into her pocket for and not found. And she couldn't see out of the box, poor Mother. She couldn't see him looking in at her from this outside now. She'd gone on putting on the pale-blue uniform and writing on the form as if the studies would go on, as if the world would stay safe enough for babies to arrive and be measured. The little, clean-dressed Sheegeh, he had never been really surprised when all that scrubbing and polishing of things had failed, but of course he had often been dirty in his life, whereas Mother and Father had not. It was all a big shock to them.

"We'll run out of light," said Doppo. Sheegeh rolled up the tape. He put it in an inside pocket and went on with the hunt.

You catch the baby, Mother had said, in the underground room. That one had been quite spacious too, and neat, full of good-quality salvage and with food stacked all up the walls.

Like a football! Sheegeh had laughed.

More like a . . . Like when the ferry comes in and the man runs up and puts the ramp across, and the ropes. Like a ceremony, or a—

Anyway, Father said heavily from the corner.

Well, said Mother, *you check this and that and the other, and one of the things you check is the circumference of the head.*

Couldn't you see if it was very much too big or too small? said Sheegeh.

Yes, but it has to be on the form, to show the doc-
tor, who might not see the baby. And also, studies of
birth size . . . to show whether women from near in-
dustry or electricity, or who smoke—

It got complicated after that, and Sheegeh
must have stopped listening, because he couldn't
remember any more.

"You know what they're doing while we hunt,"
said Doppo.

Sheegeh shrugged off Doppo's oncoming
words.

"They brought back girls, you know. Didn't
you see? No, of course not—they don't let you see
the girls, for fear your golden hair might fall out
with the shock. Well, they did, and now they're
warrumping those girls. Everyone's having a go,
one girl after the other, one Duwazza after the
other."

Sheegeh watched Doppo rage, rage against
being too young even to want to go warrumping,
rage at having to go out with Sheegeh on this pretend errand, when the house was overflowing with
loot and there'd never been a time when hunting
was less needed.

"And so?" said Sheegeh. "Why would you
want to sit around and watch that?"

Doppo turned on him. "It's only that they're
not so perfect and so pure as you seem to think,

Angel's-Arse. Even that Michael—he'll be doing it along with the rest. He's no better—he just smiles more."

Sheegeh watched Doppo empurple himself. Did Doppo's rage fit these circumstances? It didn't help that Sheegeh was not quite clear what war-rumping was. He had thought it was a walloping, a beating, which he already knew the Duwazza did, on and on until the person died and then some, but this was clearly something worse. It sounded like some kind of awful violent dance, warrumping, maybe with Fat Owen beating out the music for it on the bottom of an emptied fire-drum, working up a sweat, the light on his glasses making him look blind.

"Anyway," said Sheegeh, "if they've sent us away, they must have good reason, is all I know. It's surely something that we don't need to see or do."

They came back to the Duwazza house toward evening. Gayorg, Chechin, and Michael had the fire going in the holey drum outside. Sheegeh was glad of it. The nights were beginning to nip now.

"Hey-hey, Angel-Face," they said when they saw him, "come here and let me feel your lucky hair."

Sheegeh let them stroke his head and tug his curls for luck—it hurt, but it was what he was here for, what they used him for, and better than what they used a lot of people for. Somewhere where he kept his thoughts from going, Sheegeh knew he was lucky.

Having had his bowl of the stew, he did not stay by the drum. He went inside and fetched the notebook from his bedroll, and the pencil. He stuck them in his coat and climbed up the rubble to where he could step over onto the house roof. He kept to the parts over the ceiling joists. The tin scraped fearsomely on the nails, and people shouted, first inside, then out at the drum. "It's only me!" Sheegeh called out, and they were silent, until he showed his golden head to their view, and then they relaxed, seeing no one with a gun to his throat or temple, or more likely a knife these days.

"What do you mean, scaring the squitters out of people?" shouted Doppo.

"Be quiet," said Gayorg. "He's our angel; he can go anywhere he wants."

Doppo grumbled something.

Sheegeh crossed to the Guardian on the roof. The half-man had been wired up here like a scarecrow, a long time ago. All his flesh was shriveled to leather, and no longer stank. He had one of the old tin helmets on, jauntily angled. Sheegeh took that off and laid it on the roof.

"Don't you fall down," Michael called out. "You can't really fly, you know, spite of your feathery wings."

Down there they all laughed. But Sheegeh

wasn't going to fall—there was no such likelihood. He took out the tape and put it around the head so that he could see the measurement by the firelight on the forehead.

"Fifty-five point two." He rolled up the tape and put it back in his pocket.

He sat and dangled his legs over the door, and took out the pencil and notebook. Starting a new page, he wrote *55.2 cm.* "Hey, what's the date today?" he called down.

Michael took a newspaper out of his back pants pocket. "Yesterday was Wednesday the seventeenth of October," he said. "Today I didn't manage a paper."

Sheegeh wrote the date next to the measurement. *Man on house roof,* he wrote beside it, which filled the line to the end with a little cramping. Someone came out the door, bumped his legs, and knocked the pencil off the end of the last word. "Aargh," Sheegah said. "Look where you're going."

"Look where you're hanging your feet," said Hyram, rubbing his head.

Sheegeh stood again and picked up the helmet. When he put it back on the man, though, something gave way underneath. He was just in time to catch the face of the thing.

"Whoops!" said someone down below.

Doppo shouted, "What did you think would happen, fiddling with that?"

"Stay there, Angel," said Gayorg. "I'll come up and fix it back on."

The nose bones were sharp in Sheegeh's hands. He turned the head over to sit in its helmet, like a pudding in a bowl.

"Always showing off," said Doppo.

"You're just jealous you don't have magic hair," someone said.

"Why would I want girlie hair like that?"

There was a moment's quiet, then Chechin said easily, "Yeah, it'd look pretty silly around your grogan face."

Which was too true for anyone to answer.

"Here." Gayorg crossed the roof, grinding and squeaking the tin on the nails much worse than Sheegeh had. "Give us it. I've been wanting to do this for ages—tuck his head under his arm. I know just how."

Sheegeh surrendered the head, held the wire that Gayorg took off the hand, then gave it back to him and stepped back down the roof. He put the notebook and pencil back in his bed, then went out to warm his hands at one of the drum-holes and watch the flames poking out of them like horns or pointy orange tongues.

Sometimes when Sheegeh hadn't had enough sleep, his mind slumped straight from waking into a dream. All the noise of the Duwazza around him would fade to silence—it was a silent dream. And he could not make himself heard; the people were too far away. He stood on cleared ground and watched them come toward him across the mounds of rubble. The first—was it her?—came slowly, picking her way carefully, because she was wearing a pale-blue uniform and those soft white shoes. She hadn't seen him yet. He was almost sure it was her. And the man behind, even slower, watched his feet in their pinching shiny shoes find a way down the treacherous rubble. Neither of them had given up hope of staying clean, of arriving without mishap at the cleared ground. They didn't know as Sheegeh did that you throw yourself at such piles, spread yourself wide, scramble fast so that even if something does dislodge, you're already past it, you don't fall with it. You're always covered with brick dust, but so is everything, and everyone, so what matter?

He watched them in silence, but he never could decide enough that it was really them, to explode and run at them. *Somebody's* clean mother, *somebody's* dressed-up father, were coming, but the worst thing in the world would be to run to them, to let go and shout and start scrambling, and then look up and see that the faces were strange, that these were someone else's people, just like everyone else in the world.

He wouldn't do that to himself. He would stand here and wait for them to be close enough, to be sure.

And he always woke while he waited. He might have just taken a first nearly sure step or opened his mouth and drawn breath ready. She might have just slipped a little and checked the state of her skirt with familiar hands, a familiar anxious angling of her head. The man might have just lifted his face, seeming to smile at Sheegeh, seeming to easily recognize him.

And then he would be back in the Duwazza house, with everybody rugged up and murmuring, or maybe Gayorg singing his Gayorgian songs with the words that mysteriously made everyone laugh—everyone but Doppo, who pretended to laugh anyway, and Sheegeh himself. If they saw Sheegeh awake, someone jokingly put hands over his innocent ears. Or he would be out in the firelit cold, with two boys wrestling, and his stomach growling, and the spotter beam crawling all over the low cloud, as if enemies came from above instead of dwelling right down here among them.

He was alone, in the old park, a bald, cratered place, the trees long gone for firewood, the circles and rectangles of flower beds marked out, built up, the curved-wire path borders going from nowhere to nowhere, looking like safe ways marked across a mined place, or sown explosives themselves, conspicuous so as to warn people not to flee here into worse danger.

There was a muddy dog with him—or around

WAR IS . . .

him, anyway—printing its own patterns on the patterned ground.

The dog went into a crater and nudged something on the bottom with its nose: a gray body, in gray clothing, lying in gray water. When the dog moved it, Sheegeh discerned the top of a head, with black hair slicked across and coming away, and he veered down into the crater. He knelt and took the tape out of his pocket, lifted the head and slipped the tape underneath to measure it at the widest part.

He shooed the dog away, which had waded into the water and was bumping the body looking for a good part to eat.

There was a man in the hills somewhere, he'd heard, behind where the ski jump had been, among those rich houses that were all but leveled now, the owners gone just while the forces were fighting in the parliament, before even a shot had been fired. The Duwazza hated those owners; the Duwazza had taken every scrap of loot, whole or broken, from those house shells long ago, before Sheegeh's time.

Anyway, this man, Owen said (Owen was disgusted by it), he went around collecting dogs.

What, to eat? Doppo had said.

No, to mind. *To look after. Not only finds the dogs, but finds food for the dogs. Cooks 'em up big vats of the stuff. Keeps 'em in a big pen up there, hundreds o' these flea-bit rag-dogs you see around the place.*

That's good, isn't it? someone had said doubt-fully from behind Sheegeh. *Being kind to animals?*

When there are people *starving? People without houses? To care about* dogs?

Yeah, why not?

'Cause it's soppy and it's wrong. People *first,* then *the dogs and the horses and the budgies and the . . . you know?*

"Fifty-seven exactly." Sheegeh noted it in the book. *In crater, M. W. Memorial Park.*

He got up and walked up the slope again, tucking away the notebook and drying the back of the tape on his coat. Behind him the dog *clomped* on something, began to gnaw. Between the scrap-ing noises were bits of voice, bits of whine, bits of *yum.* It was good not to mind anymore. It was good to be used to these things.

He had found the Duwazza by accident, wandered onto their ground soon after the world had stopped making sense, looked up from his hunting and they were ranged around on the rubble piles as if in a theater—still, dark-clothed, some of them smok-ing. He remembered thinking, *I must get some kind of woolly for my head like that*—Gayorg, it had been, wearing it—because at that time too the weather had been gathering itself for winter. So it must be a year ago now.

"Hey, Angel-Face," said one, who would later become Michael. "Can you do us a favor?" He asked in such a friendly voice that it didn't occur to Sheegeh to refuse, even though there were so many watching.

"What?"

"Can you hold some stones for us?"

Sheegeh didn't answer because the request seemed too strange. He stood and thought how handsome Michael was—thin, like most people, but how his eyes stayed steady on you instead of switching away, and were full of kindness.

Michael picked up two stones, slithered down the mound, and stood. He held a stone in each hand, his arms out at either side of him. "Just like this," he said. "Can you do that?"

Sheegeh nodded.

"Out to here." Michael strode out to Sheegeh and beyond him, where the ground was even flatter. Sheegeh followed. "Right here," said Michael, and he turned to face the others and put out his arms with the stones again.

Sheegeh stood beside him and put his arms out.

"Look straight back at us," said Michael.

The others were not very much different from corpses, lying there, but a head was raised here, those shoulders were hunched as corpses' never were, a foot tapped. Bored as they were, they were full of thoughts and little movements.

"Keep looking," said Michael. He threw away one of the stones and took a different one out of his pocket, and put it in Sheegeh's hand.

"That's a funny one," Sheegeh said amiably.

"It *is* a funny one," said Michael. "Don't look," he added, "but you can feel it."

Sheegeh felt the lighter stone. "Pattern of squares," he said.

Michael was between him and the stone. He looked at Sheegeh over his shoulder. "Yup. I just have to adjust something. Now, you just stand there very still, when I go. Don't squeeze the stones; don't drop them; don't let them flop by your side. Just hold them out and stand there. All right?"

"All right." It was nice to hear a kind voice, telling him what to do. It was a relief. He knew it was Duwazza, but not all Duwazza were so gentle.

Michael held his hand around the stone and made a sound there as if slicing part of the stone off with a single knife stroke. "Good," he said. "Stay exactly like that." He leaped away toward the other boys. They were all sitting up now, and looking out at Sheegeh.

Sheegeh looked back. He did just as Michael had told him. Michael went higher than the other boys up the rubble and crouched there. He didn't move, though the others kept having little impatient spasms, unfolding, folding back up, staring, waving their arms. A voice called out, "Squeeze it!"

then "Squeeze them both!" but because it was not Michael's voice, Sheegeh did not do so.

The sky was low and gray, with seams of silver sunlight throbbing through it. A breeze trickled through the place; Sheegeh couldn't see it because there were no trees, no cloths, no blowing rubbish; he could only feel his own coat edge gently bumping the back of his knees. A bird came down, black, with a sticking-up tail; it bounced down onto a brick, eyed him, flaunted its tail one way and another, bounced—*boint, boint, boint*—away from him, then took itself off again. Sheegeh was good; his arms were getting tired, but he stayed where he was told.

Then someone ran toward him, one of the bigger boys. As he got closer, Sheegeh saw that he didn't have Michael's kind face, that in fact he had an ugly, injured, bristling face. But it was all right; Michael was watching; Michael had clearly told him to come.

"Here, giss that," he said. Sheegeh gave him nothing, but he came and took the strange stone. He started walking back with it. "Yeah, it's a dud," he called to the others. "It's got that same look as the ones we got from Throwbrow's." And he strolled back, gently tossing the stone into the air, gently catching it.

Would it be all right now to lower his arms? Sheegeh wondered. Some of the boys leaned back on the pile of rubble; some of them scrambled; all of them put up their hands as if to warn the ugly boy off.

Bang! The stone blew up and the ugly boy fell. Silence packed itself into Sheegeh's ears. The cloud of the explosion passed upward and was lost against the sky.

Sheegeh came from one side and the Duwazza from the other to look at the dead ugly boy. By now, Sheegeh was used to seeing all kinds of bodies, fresh and not so fresh. This one was not too bad. He regarded the bright color of the peeled head in the middle of all this grayness.

Some of the Duwazza came around to his side to properly examine the boy.

"He's not gonna wake up and start moaning, is he?" said one unhappily. This was a boy Doppo's age who Sheegeh never learned the name of; he had woken up screaming of stomach pains two nights later. The Duwazza had carried him off to the Red Cross doctors, and Sheegeh had not seen him since.

"No, no," said Michael. "Not with that head."

"Good," said the boy, then added swaggeringly, "'cause I hate it when they do that."

Michael felt the ugly boy's wrist. "Nada," he said, dropping it, and then he straightened up, and got out tobacco in a packet. He rolled himself a cigarette fast, with one hand, lit it with a pink plastic lighter, and put everything away. Now he was looking at Sheegeh.

"So you were lucky, eh? You're still here."

Sheegeh kept his eyes on the ugly boy, in case the ugly boy was popular and people were angry with Sheegeh for killing him.

"We can give him another, make him do it again," said someone.

"He's lucky, not stupid." Michael came and touched Sheegeh's hair. "The whole point is him *not* knowing what the stone does. Isn't it, Angel-Hair? Look at this golden fluff. How do you keep it so clean? You go to the beauty parlor?"

He was joking in a kindly way, and Sheegeh pulled his mouth down in a smile and shook his head.

Which is how it all began with the Duwazza. They took him to their house and he was theirs. Michael gave an order that no one was to touch any part of him but his hair, so they washed that and combed it like a doll's and marveled at how it curled up again as it dried. They ran their fingers through it when they were all kitted up for a raid, for luck, and he would stay there with Fat Owen, who was an encumbrance but loyal and could cook. They would sleep until the Duwazza came back in, either wild with weapons and loot or silent with things they had seen. Sheegeh would wake, watch, listen to check that his luck still held, and go back to sleep until morning.

. . .

He walked down the safe street. They called it Dresses Street, because for a long time two of the shop windows stayed good, one full of bridal gowns, one of evening gowns. People had broken the glass themselves and taken the gowns, eventually, for the cloth, and the brides' wooden dummies for fuel. Most of the metal ones were still in the evening-gown shop, though, woman-shaped cages on metal stalks, straighter-backed and more confident than any woman walked anymore.

The day before yesterday, Dresses Street had not been safe, and there were the bodies to prove it, fallen quite neatly against the walls they had thought would shelter them. They were still good, with the cold—there was no smell. Boots and coats had been taken, so they lay rather vulnerable in cardigans, T-shirts. One of the younger women wore nothing at all, so Sheegeh didn't look lower than her head. Her reddish curls made her hard to measure, so he put a question mark and the words *thick hair* beside his measurement.

He went zigzag up the street with his tape and book. It was quiet, so early; it was the hour when the city seemed to catch its breath and stretch its cramped limbs *just* a little, but not enough to catch the eye of anyone with a weapon. There was just the rustle of the tape, the crack of the notebook cover as he wrote against his knee, and the whisper of the pencil on the paper.

■ ■ ■

　　　　　　　　　　　WAR IS . . .

"Look what Gayorg brought me," said Sheegeh, holding up the textbook.

Fat Owen squinted at it. The room was dim, with only two candles, the windows blacked out with plywood and duct tape so as not to attract fire. "My heaven," said Owen, "I've seen that before, I think. Hang on, let me . . ."

He pushed some chopped thing off a board into the soup, stirred it, and came to the table. "Ah, my, yes. *Math Challenge*. The green one—that's for older kids than you, I think. Let me see." He took the book and opened it in a couple of places.

"Does it make any sense to you?" said Sheegeh. "I tried before. I can sound out the words, but . . ."

"You need the yellow one," said Owen. He opened the cover, where all the books were shown. "See? Right up here, to start with. This book is way down *here*—you have to know everything that's in all *these* books before you can tackle this one—"

A shell exploded nearby. The house shook. Some dust trickled off a rafter and sparkled and spat in the candle flame. Owen looked around. When the house didn't break anywhere, he went back to the book, pushing his glasses up his nose.

Sheegeh slumped at the table. "I guess Gayorg's not going to be able to find all the others. Can you understand this one?"

"Oh, I did all this. This is cinchy for me. I was

onto the serious books, where they didn't color them up and make them look fun, put in those little pictures. I was crunching hard numbers. I was going to be an aeronautical engineer."

"I don't even know what that is," said Sheegeh. "You were good at school, huh?"

"I had to be," said Owen, "if I wasn't good at running or football, hey." He sat and leafed fondly through the pages.

"Do me one of these triangles?" Sheegeh asked. "Show me that first one."

"I need something to write on."

"I've got that." Sheegeh fetched his notebook and pencil.

Owen opened it at the page-and-a-half of Sheegeh's head measurements. "This your work? Hmm, that's a good sign, liking numbers."

He opened a clean pair of pages and did the first task in the book. "I'll do it, then I'll see if I can explain it." He laid down neat codes on Sheegeh's page, all his bulk concentrated on their neatness and rightness, muttering to himself the language of the book. "So it's sixty-two degrees, that one," he said, sitting back after a little while. "Right, first you've got to understand some things about triangles."

Sheegeh tried to listen, but he was distracted by the picture in his mind of them sitting there in the lamplight and the soup smell, Owen helping him, all cozy in the middle of the night's darkness and the battle noise.

"You see what I'm saying?" said Owen.

Sheegeh shook his head. "Tell me again," he said. *And this time I'll listen properly,* he added to himself.

And Owen did tell him. Owen was that sort of boy. How he'd managed to get caught up by the Duwazza, Sheegeh couldn't imagine. Usually the Duwazza were not very nice to fat people.

In a ravaged place, looking for shelter from the rain, they came to a room full of cots, in each a withered child. Doppo went along the metal cupboards, making a great clash and rattle, talking his head off. "There might be medical supplies here," he said. Then, "Someone's been through this place already. But they might have left something, if they were in a hurry. Some bandages, maybe, some drugs. Gayorg likes his drugs, doesn't he? Likes boiling up his little cong-coctions?"

"He will kill himself one day," said Sheegeh, repeating what he'd heard Michael say. He had hooked his armpits over a cot rail and was measuring the first head. And wasn't it little! Only thirty-six point one!

And there were so many in here! He skipped past Owen's triangle work and started a new page. *Cot Room,* he called it, and drew a plan marking the door they'd come in at and eighteen rectangles for the cots. *36.1,* he wrote in the first.

"Nothing in here, either." Doppo kicked a broken cardboard box out of the other room, making as much noise as possible. "Someone has been through thoroughly." He went to the door and gloomed; the rain was hissing down out there, slapping to the ground from broken guttering, starting to make a deep tinny gurgle in a pipe that sounded happy to funnel it, even though half the roof it took rain from was gone, and there was nowhere but a crater for the runoff to go. "It could stay like this all day," he moaned.

"It sounds as if it will." Sheegeh, across the room, stood next to an empty cot and wrote *empty* in its rectangle in the notebook. In each occupied cot, pale brownness stained the mattress where the fluids had soaked in, like a decorative border drawn specifically to the shape of that child. Sheegeh tried to move the heads as little as possible. When he took away the tape, he made sure each head faced the same way as before, that it sat in the little dent its own weight had made in the mattress, when it had had weight.

"We're not proper Duwazza," Michael had said bitterly—in the summer it must have been, because the candlelight had shone on Michael's rolled-up sleeves, in the hair on his arm next to Sheegeh at the table, and on his shaven head.

They'd all shaven their heads in the summer, to stop the itching that had been driving them mad. Only Sheegeh had been allowed to keep a token lock, like a little tail on the back of his head. Michael himself had picked the louse eggs out of that.

"We are, too, proper!" Chechin had sounded insulted.

Michael snorted. "Duwazza used to be *men*. I saw them. Kids like Doppo would hang around and they would laugh at them and send them away—they didn't need them. They had uniforms. They had weapons, and all the weapons matched. They had an organization, with proper cells, and membership papers and runners and passwords and executions. This, what we've got now. . . ." He looked around at them, and Sheegeh watched their faces close down, except for the one or two that were angry.

"This is just kids playing in the ruins," said Michael. "Not just the city ruins. The ruins of the Duwazza, too. I mean, apart from the mob at the university, who do we organize with? Who do we even *know*, since Temprance and Spek and their boys got theirs? It's almost just us, the last little remnant. *In*glorious, it is. An *in*glorious end."

Sheegeh didn't quite follow him—wasn't *glorious* a good thing? He looked across the table at Gayorg, who could often say the thing that made everyone feel better.

Gayorg was looking back at Michael. His hand snuck up to the table as if he were trying to hide its action even from himself and deposited one of his yellow pills there, a shiny flattened oval. It rocked there on the tabletop, and Gayorg watched it. Sheegeh could see him enjoying the sight, enjoying the anticipation.

"I think we do pretty good," said Chechin hotly.

As Chechin started ticking off their deeds on his fingers, Gayorg, low over the happy pill, lifted his eyes and looked straight across at Sheegeh. His eyebrows slowly lifted, and a sweet, wondering smile crept onto his face. Just below his chin, the little pill rocked and shone out its promise.

And so it was with some semblance of a uniform that they lined up for their raids now. Chechin had found the black cloth after that summer night. It was patterned with flowers, but they were black too, woven in, and would be invisible in the dark. There was enough for everyone except the newest boy to have a new wrap for his head.

Tonight they went in late. Sheegeh stayed up later than usual, so that he would be there at the door when they left, and each could touch his hair on the way out. Doppo was with them this time; Doppo looked scornfully out of the slit in his head wrap and trotted past Sheegeh without touching.

"Hup!" said the boy behind him. "Back here."

"I don't need his *luck,*" said Doppo over his shoulder.

The boy went after him and brought him back. "You want to kill us all?" he said, banging Doppo's stiffened hand onto Sheegeh's curls and rubbing hard. "You want to be the hole in our defense?"

He let go, and Doppo snatched back his hand. The other boy's eyes rolled and he rubbed Sheegeh's curls more gently. "Some people think they're indestructible, don't they, Angel-Face?"

When they'd gone, Fat Owen said, "Triangles? Nah, too late for triangles. Look at you." But he sat up himself with *Math Challenge,* writing his workings on pieces of foreign newspaper where the advertising pictures left good stretches of the page blank.

Sheegeh woke to see Owen lift his head from his arms on the table. The candle was dead, but there was first light outside. There was a stumbling sound, a rattle of rubble, a wounded moan. Owen heaved up and hurried to open the door.

"Mother Mary!" He came back to the table and fumbled to light a fresh candle.

The new boy filled the doorway, with someone else—Brisk, one of their biggest—around his shoulders. "They're all gone," said the new boy. "Every one. Except us." He lowered Brisk to stand and propped him there.

"What? Come in!" said Owen. "Get him onto the bunk there. Let us look at him."

"No, no," said Brisk. "It's too bad. Don't touch me. Just lay me down." His vinyl jacket was buttoned all up and down. A row of blood drips was gathering at the bottom edge, running along, dripping from the corner.

They helped him across the floor and sagged him onto the lower bunk, which was Michael's, with Gayorg's above.

Owen went for the buttons. "Now, let's—"

Brisk pushed him away. Both Brisk's hands were washed and washed again with dried blood. "I just wanted to die at home," he said, "'stead of out there, on the ground." Something inside the jacket made a soggy sound. "It won't take long," he said.

Owen caught one of the hands wandering on the chest of the jacket. "You take as long as you like, Brisk," he said. "We'll try and make you comfortable." He brought the big hand up to his teeth and cried on it, silently.

The new boy swayed, holding himself up by the bunk frame, staring down at Brisk.

"Cobbla brought me home," said Brisk, but his lungs were seriously disturbed now, groaning and bubbling blood up onto his lips.

Sheegeh remembered Michael saying once, *It's a home. It's got kids in it.*

Yeah, Doppo had said, looking pleased.

Not you. Gayorg had given him a push. *Innocent kids. Angel.*

And Doppo had looked at Sheegeh with open dislike.

"Cobbla's a good man." Brisk coughed up a last gout of blood. It spread its red shine down his chin, and his noisy breathing stopped.

Owen closed Brisk's eyes and positioned his hands on his chest. Then he heaved himself up, his wet face grave.

"No one else?" he said to Cobbla.

"They all got—they all—"

"Show us," said Owen. "Take us there. Sheegeh?"

Sheegeh was already dressing. *Owen never called me Sheegeh before,* he thought. *Owen never called me anything—not Angel, or Angel-Hair, or Angel-Face or anything.*

Owen was going through everything in the hut. "Can you use this? Do you want this?" he said to Cobbla. "Here, you can swap these for something useful, maybe." He put together a pack full of foodstuffs, and pots and utensils. "Here." He passed Sheegeh Michael's pack. "Put a layer of mixed tins in the bottom of that, like mine, and fill up the rest with the good blankets."

They covered Brisk with a couple of the thinner, more holed blankets, and went out, laden, into the silent city. Cobbla led them. Owen couldn't move fast, couldn't climb over things, so

Cobbla took them the way he'd brought Brisk. It was still not fully light, and Sheegeh fancied that every dark mark on the ground was Brisk's blood, dripped from his coat edge on the way home.

He had thought Cobbla was lying—Cobbla just had a lying way about him. Then he saw them, and thought, *Now they're dead. This time they're dead.* They were scattered across the mound just like the first time he'd seen them, but motionless, with their heads downward, as if the black wraps had made their heads so heavy that they had dragged them down the slope.

"Up there in the arch," said Cobbla, pointing up at the one remaining wall of the stadium. "Someone had a *machine gun* up there. They just waited and picked their moment and swept and swept. They all got mown down. I was just lucky. I just saw it happening up the other end, and I just got down in a lucky place—down there, see?— and I could get away bit by bit in between sweeps. I seen them. They was soldiers, or someone pretending to be soldiers."

He went on, as if his voice had gotten unblocked somehow and now couldn't be stopped. He described how Brisk had fallen and where, how he'd fetched Brisk and gotten Brisk out.

Sheegeh shrugged off his pack and went up the slope. The stadium wall shaded the whole rubble mound cold blue-gray from the dawning sky.

He started a new page: *Duwazza.* He had to

unwrap every head; once he had measured, he covered the face with the black-flowered cloth. Christos and Melon had *thick hair*. Chechin's skull was *broken left side,* where he'd fallen on a corner of brick with some force. After Doppo, when the tape was soft and delicate and stained from Doppo's head ooze, Sheegeh felt his face contracted into a pig face against the tears. He breathed in the tear-snot through his nose, held it there, and breathed out through his mouth, going "Uh" each time, moving from boy to boy, from head to head up the slope.

The tape didn't come apart until he was oh-so-carefully rolling it up to put away in his pocket. He'd thought, *It'll dry there from the warmth of me, and probably be as good as new.* Now he stood with the rolled piece on his fingers with its soggy red end, and the loose piece in his other hand, and he didn't know what he thought. He didn't know how much use it was now; in the old days he might have taped it together and used it again—but in the old days he wouldn't be doing this, would he, measuring dead heads? He could use the longer part, perhaps, and then do the sum, adding— he checked: twelve-point-eight. Adding twelve-point-eight . . . No, you'd start at thirteen. Adding thirteen . . .

He put both pieces in his pocket. You never know, he might find himself in the kind of place that had tape. He came back down to Owen and

Cobbla, who were sitting on the packs at the foot of the mound.

"They all there?" said Owen.

Sheegeh sat on his own pack and handed Owen the open notebook. The page was a little messy with blood smudges.

Owen read the name column aloud from top to bottom, slowly. Even for Michael, his voice didn't shake; Sheegeh admired him greatly. It was almost like a proper funeral.

While he read, Cobbla was leaning in to see the page. When Owen had finished, Cobbla touched the other column with his little finger. "What's these?"

"Their head measurements. The circumference," said Owen.

"*Head* measurements? That's what he was doing up there all that time? Measuring their heads? What's the point of—"

"He measures. Their heads," said Owen loudly and soberly. "That's. What he does," said Owen. "You want to go through their pockets, be my guest. Bring me any papers you find."

Cobbla was already up the slope. "Head measurements!" floated down to them as he bent to the first body.

Owen handed back Sheegeh's notebook. "I thought I might look out one of those camps," he said, "seeing I've got no one to raid for me anymore. The one close to us, by Pontoon Bridge, I've heard they will take you if you wait long enough outside, even though they say they are turning people away. And I can wait." He patted the pack underneath him, patted his own belly, sending out ripples.

Sheegeh gave a stiff little nod. He looked at the ground and then up at Owen's round, harmless face and down again.

"Hey, I'm not mad about this Cobbla," Owen said low. "Reckon you could come along with me and keep an eye on him?"

"As if I could do anything, *my* size," Sheegeh said to his lap.

"I could sit on him, and you could knock him out with—I don't know, half a brick? A tin o' beans?"

Sheegeh's whole chest was full of sharp hardnesses. He didn't want to disappoint Owen.

"What? You've another plan?" Owen sounded amused. "Skip off to Paree? Open a little beestro?"

"Go up to Grandview," said Sheegeh.

Owen stopped chuckling. "Grandview? There's no pickings up there anymore—you will starve once you're through your tins, if you're not robbed of them on the way."

"I want to find that dog man, that you told us about," Sheegeh said, apologizing. "See what he's up to."

Owen stared at him and blinked.

"Hoo-hoo!" Cobbla stood over Michael's body, waving a banded roll of currency.

"He might not even be there anymore," said Owen. "That dog man. It was a while ago I heard that."

Sheegeh shrugged. "I'll see if he is. If he's not, I'll come back down and try a camp like you." He stood up.

Owen watched him unfasten the pack. "Pontoon Bridge is good. I hear they've got a school there, even, for your-age kids."

Sheegeh took out a good blanket and put it on Cobbla's pack. He took out another and gave it to Owen, who took it, looking stricken, and hugged it. "You be careful going across town," he said. "Go now—go early. And hide when things start to wake up."

"Don't worry." Sheegeh tied up the pack and shouldered it and shook Owen's hand. His face was cold and tight with the drying tears, his eyelashes clumped with them.

He had to watch his feet as he walked away, stepping over the scattered concrete chunks and brick bits.

"Keep up with your triangles, eh," said Owen.

Sheegeh turned and smiled to show he'd heard. From here, Cobbla seemed to float above Owen, bent over and rummaging in a sprawled shadow.

"I will," Sheegeh said, and walked on.

WAR IS...

FURTHER READING

**COPYRIGHT
ACKNOWLEDGMENTS**

FURTHER READING

There are whole libraries filled with books about war—fiction, plays, poetry, and nonfiction from ancient times to the present—though overwhelmingly the books are aimed at adults. This bibliography suggests some works about war that have special appeal for teens. Some are by the authors included in this anthology, both works that we have quoted (as indicated by asterisks) and also other books by these writers that focus on war. We have included in addition books by a selected group of other young adult and adult authors whose works need to be acknowledged in any basic introductory reading list on war. In the case of classics, we have given recent editions. Paperback and audio editions may be available. We also encourage readers to look through adult anthologies as starting points that will lead to more writings of all kinds on this most fascinating and important subject for human discourse.

ANTHOLOGIES

Forché, Carolyn, ed. *Against Forgetting: Twentieth-Century Poetry of Witness.* New York: Norton, 1993.

Keegan, John. *The Book of War: 25 Centuries of Great War Writing.* New York: Penguin, 1999.

FICTION

ANCIENT WARS

Fleischman, Paul. *Dateline: Troy.* Revised edition. Cambridge, MA: Candlewick, 2006. [YA]

Lattimore, Richard, trans. *The Iliad of Homer.* University of Chicago Press, 1961.

Pressfied, Steven. *Gates of Fire: An Epic Novel of the Battle of Thermopylae*. New York: Doubleday, 1998.

NAPOLEONIC WARS

Holub, Josef. *An Innocent Soldier*. Michael Hofmann, trans. New York: Scholastic/Arthur A. Levine, 2005. [YA]

Tolstoy, Leo. *War and Peace*. Constance Garnett, trans. New York: Random House/Modern Library, 2002.

AMERICAN REVOLUTIONARY WAR

Elliott, L. M. *Give Me Liberty*. New York: HarperCollins/Katherine Tegen, 2006. [YA]

AMERICAN CIVIL WAR

Crane, Stephan. *The Red Badge of Courage*. Mineola, NY: Dover, 2004.

Fleischman, Paul. *Bull Run*. New York: HarperCollins, 1993. [YA]

Mitchell, Margaret. *Gone with the Wind*. New York: Scribner, 2007.

Paulsen, Gary. *Soldier's Heart: A Novel of the Civil War*. New York: Delacorte. 1998. [YA]

Wells, Rosemary. *Red Moon at Sharpsburg*. New York: Viking, 2007. [YA]

WORLD WAR I

Hamley, Dennis. *Without Warning: Ellen's Story, 1914–1918*. Cambridge, MA: Candlewick, 2007. [YA]

Morpugo, Michael. *Private Peaceful*. New York: Scholastic, 2004. [YA]

Remarque, Erich Maria. *All Quiet on the Western Front.* New York: Ballantine, 1996.

Sedgwick, Marcus. *The Foreshadowing.* New York: Random House/Wendy Lamb, 2006. [YA]

WORLD WAR II
Cormier, Robert. *Heroes.* New York: Delacorte, 1998. [YA]

Heller, Joseph. *Catch-22: A Novel.* New York: Simon & Schuster, 1999.

Hughes, Dean. *Soldier Boys.* New York: Atheneum, 2001. [YA]

Lawrence, Iain. *B for Buster.* New York: Delacorte, 2004. [YA]

Mazer, Harry. *A Boy at War: A Novel of Pearl Harbor.* New York: Simon & Schuster, 2001. [YA]

———. *A Boy No More.* New York: Simon & Schuster, 2004. [YA]

———. *Heroes Don't Run: A Novel of the Pacific War.* New York: Simon & Schuster, 2005. [YA]

———. *The Last Mission.* New York: Delacorte, 1979. [YA]

Salisbury, Graham. *Eyes of the Emperor.* New York: Random House/Wendy Lamb, 2005. [YA]

———. *Under the Blood-Red Sun.* New York: Delacorte, 1994. [YA]

Wiesel, Elie. *Night.* New York: Hill and Wang, 2006.

VIETNAM WAR
Kadohata, Cynthia. *Cracker! The Best Dog in Vietnam.* New York: Atheneum, 2007. [YA]

Myers, Walter Dean. *Fallen Angels.* New York: Scholastic, 1988. [YA]

———. *Patrol: An American Soldier in Vietnam.* Illus. by Ann Grifalconi. New York: HarperCollins, 2001.

O'Brien, Tim. *Going after Cacciato.* New York: Doubleday, 1978.

———. *The Things They Carried.* Boston: Houghton Mifflin, 1990.

SOMALIA
*Bauman, Christian. *The Ice Beneath You.* New York: Scribner, 2002.

AFGHANISTAN
Ellis, Deborah. *The Breadwinner.* Toronto: Douglas & McIntyre/Groundwood, 2001. [YA]

Jolin, Paula. *In the Name of God.* New Milford, CT: Roaring Brook, 2007.

IRAQ
*Bellavia, David. *House to House.* New York: Free Press, 2007.

Myers, Walter Dean. *Sunrise Over Fallujah.* New York: Scholastic, 2008. [YA]

RWANDAN GENOCIDE
Stassen, Jean-Philippe. *Deogratias, a Tale of Rwanda.* Alex Siegel, trans. New York: First Second, 2006. [graphic novel]

IMAGINARY WARS

Card, Orson Scott. *Ender's Game.* New York: Tor, 1992.

Cormier, Robert. *After the First Death.* New York: Pantheon, 1979. [YA]

Marsden, John. *Tomorrow When the War Began.* Boston: Houghton Mifflin, 1995. [YA]

Rosoff, Meg. *How I Live Now.* New York: Random House/Wendy Lamb, 2004. [YA]

NONFICTION

THINKING ABOUT WAR

Allison, Aimee, and David Solnit. *Army of None: Strategies to Counter Military Recruitment, End War, and Build a Better World.* New York: Seven Stories Press, 2007.

*Hedges, Chris. *War Is a Force That Gives Us Meaning.* New York: Public-Affairs, 2002.

*———. *What Every Person Should Know About War.* New York: Free Press, 2003.

Sun Tzu. *The Art of War.* Lionel Giles, trans. Mineola, NY: Dover, 2002. [Spark Publishing, 2003. Audio 2005. Barnes & Noble, 2004. Translated by Cloud Hands. Cloud Hands Press, 2004.]

AMERICAN CIVIL WAR

McPherson, James M. *Fields of Fury: The American Civil War.* New York: Atheneum, 2002.

Murphy, Jim. *The Boys' War: Confederate and Union Soldiers Talk About the Civil War.* New York: Clarion, 1990. [YA]

WORLD WAR II

Bartoletti, Susan Campbell. *Hitler Youth: Growing Up in Hitler's Shadow*. New York: Scholastic, 2005. [YA]

Hersey, John. *Hiroshima*. New York: Vintage, 1989.

O'Donnell, Joe. *Japan 1945: A U.S. Marine's Photographs from Ground Zero*. Nashville: Vanderbilt University Press, 2005.

*Nichols, David, ed. *Ernie's War: The Best of Ernie Pyle's World War II Dispatches*. New York: Simon & Schuster, 1987.

Sullivan, Edward T. *The Ultimate Weapon: The Race to Develop the Atomic Bomb*. Holiday House, 2007. [YA]

TERRORISM

Jacobson, Sid, and Ernie Colon. *The 9/11 Report: A Graphic Adaptation*. New York: Hill and Wang, 2006. [YA]

Meltzer, Milton. *The Day the Sky Fell: A History of Terrorism*. Revised ed. New York: Random House/Landmark Books, 2002. [YA]

CONTEMPORARY MEMOIRS

Akbar, Said Hyder, and Susan Burton. *Come Back to Afghanistan: A California Teenager's Story*. New York: Bloomsbury, 2005. [YA]

de Clercq Zubli, Rita la Fontaine. *Disguised: A Wartime Memoir*. Cambridge, MA: Candlewick, 2007. [YA]

Hampton, Wilborn. *War in the Middle East: A Reporter's Story: Black September and the Yom Kippur War*. Cambridge, MA: Candlewick, 2007.

Raddatz, Martha. *The Long Road Home: A Story of War and Family.* New York: Putnam, 2007.

Satrapi, Marjane. *Persepolis: The Story of a Childhood.* New York: Pantheon, 2003. [graphic novel]

*Turnipseed, Joel. *Baghdad Express: A Gulf War Memoir.* St. Paul, MN: Borealis Books, 2003.

Zenatti, Valérie. *When I Was a Soldier: A Memoir.* Adriana Hunter, trans. New York: Bloomsbury, 2005.

COPYRIGHT ACKNOWLEDGMENTS